D0977001

THE MAGICAL REALITY OF
NADIA

MIDDLE SCHOOL MISCHIEF

By BASSEM YOUSSEF and
CATHERINE R. DALY

Illustrated by DOUGLAS HOLGATE

Scholastic Inc.

To Nadia and Adam, the sources of
my pride, happiness, and joy.
—B.Y.

To Katie Woehr, editor extraordinaire.
—C.D.

For Kristen and everyone
at Squishy Minnie.
—D.H.

Copyright © 2021 by Little Tut, Inc.

All rights reserved. Published by Scholastic Inc., *Publishers since 1920*. SCHOLASTIC and associated logos are trademarks and/or registered trademarks of Scholastic Inc.

The publisher does not have any control over and does not assume any responsibility for author or third-party websites or their content.

No part of this publication may be reproduced, stored in a retrieval system, or transmitted in any form or by any means, electronic, mechanical, photocopying, recording, or otherwise, without written permission of the publisher. For information regarding permission, write to Scholastic Inc., Attention: Permissions Department, 557 Broadway, New York, NY 10012.

This book is a work of fiction. Names, characters, places, and incidents are either the product of the author's imagination or are used fictitiously, and any resemblance to actual persons, living or dead, business establishments, events, or locales is entirely coincidental.

ISBN 978-1-338-57229-2

1 2021

Printed in the U.S.A.   23

First edition, November 2021

Book design by Katie Fitch and Jennifer Rinaldi

Historical Advisor: Ava Forte Vitali

Special thanks to Jevon Bolden and Pelehonuamea Harman

Welcome to GRACELAND
the home of Elvis Presley

October 12

Dear Nadia,

Hope all is well with you and the Nerd Patrol. I'm loving life in Memphis. I give tours of Graceland during the day and do my Elvis impersonation at night downtown. Did you know that Elvis liked to watch three TVs at the same time? And that he loved fried peanut butter and banana sandwiches? Hope you are staying safe and continuing to collect more of those fun facts you like to share with the world.

The weather is here, wish you were amazing. (jk)

Your friend, Titi

Nadia Youssef

123 Main Street

Santa Monica CA 90406

Prologue

The magician said—no, make that squeaked—the magic words and shape-shifted back into his human form. POOF!

"Disgusting," he said. Transforming into a squirrel had not been his first choice, but if he wanted to get up to a chandelier inside Graceland, he needed to be a small, unassuming creature that was good at climbing. Unfortunately, there were very few creatures Khefren hated more than rodents. Vile, beady-eyed creatures.

But desperate times called for desperate measures. His only goal was revenge against the teacher turned tour guide. And if it took posing as a squirrel to accomplish that, so be it. After the teacher ridiculed him outside the palace—imagine the nerve, making fun of the royal magician in front of a whole crowd of people!—Khefren had banished the teacher to his own hippopotamus-shaped amulet. To the back half of the hippo, to be precise—the teacher wasn't worthy of anything but a hippo's butt.

But an elder magician had judged Khefren's actions to be unjust and had in turn trapped Khefren in the very same amulet—the front half, praise Anubis. Three thousand years he'd spent cooped up in that thing. Luckily, he and the teacher didn't have to interact. The magician was pretty sure the teacher didn't even know he had been trapped in the hippo with him.

And ever since the teacher had completed the seven problems and gotten his body back, Khefren had been free, too. The teacher didn't know that, either.

The magician headed back to his Elvis-themed hotel room and turned on the news. And there it was—the scene of the "accident" he'd orchestrated—the crushed chandelier, the broken glass, the flashing lights of the ambulances.

"Our top story tonight comes to us from Graceland," the news anchor began, "where a deranged squirrel caused massive destruction to the foyer of Elvis Presley's historic home. The rodent chewed through a cable, causing a chandelier to fall on a local tour guide and Elvis impersonator. This is an unbelievable story. We're going to you live with reporter Brenda Mannix, who is on the scene. Brenda, what can you tell us about the situation at Graceland right now?"

The magician rolled his eyes. "Just show the body bag already," he muttered.

"Thank you, George," said the reporter. "The scene here is one of complete mayhem. And it all centers around a tour guide named . . ." She motioned for someone to come into the frame. ". . . Titi! Mr. Titi, can you tell us more about your miraculous escape from certain death?"

3

The magician's jaw dropped. No one could survive a one-thousand-pound chandelier falling on top of them. Unless . . .

He grabbed a blue suede shoe-shaped pillow off the bed and threw it at the TV. How had he overlooked this? Could it be that the elder's magic that imprisoned them both had also made the teacher . . . immortal? (Khefren was immortal, too, of course. All good magicians used their magic powers to make themselves immortal. Duh.)

How would he destroy the teacher now?

The magician needed to come up with a plan, but there was one thing he had to do first. He opened up the mini fridge and grabbed a bag of roasted almonds. Sure, they were grossly overpriced, but he had to get rid of this intense craving. The side effects of shape-shifting into a squirrel were no joke.

Chapter One

Yay!" cheered Nadia as a ball swished through the basket. She raised her fist into the air. "Nothing but net, amirite?"

Adam elbowed her in the ribs. "You're cheering for the wrong team," he informed her.

"Oh," said Nadia, slightly embarrassed. It was the day before school started after the holiday break and she and her friends were sitting in the stands at their very first middle school basketball game, Bridget Mason Middle versus Tenth Street. Though they were more inclined to attend a debate tournament than a sporting event, they were there to support their newish friend Jason, who played on the team.

Nadia looked over at her freckled, redheaded best friend, who was watching the game intently. It was only a couple of months ago that Adam didn't know a goal from a touchdown. (They had goals in basketball, right?) And now, thanks to his desire to bond with his new stepdad, he was a veritable sports fanatic.

"Don't worry, Nadia," said Vikram. "You know I'm just here for the snacks." He held up a box of nachos. "Mmmmm. The cheese just melts in your mouth."

Vikram was also one of Nadia's friends. The group called themselves the Nerd Patrol, and was originally made up of Nadia, Adam, Chloe, Sarah, and Vikram. They were a diverse group. Nadia was born in Egypt; Adam had recently discovered he had roots in Austria; Vikram's parents were from India; Sarah was Korean American; and Chloe was half Jamaican American, half Barbadian American. But they had a lot in common. They were smart and funny. They took school seriously, but not necessarily themselves. They considered themselves well-rounded geeks. Even so, everyone had been surprised when Nadia suggested they go to the basketball game.

"Well, Jason is part of the Nerd Patrol now," Nadia had said. "He plays sports. We should support him!"

Nobody could argue with that.

"So this is what the jocks do on Saturday afternoons," marveled Chloe, looking around as she smoothed her velvet skirt. Nadia, unsure about what to wear to a sporting event, had gone with the safe jeans-and-T-shirt combo. But Chloe looked like she always did—a middle school fashionista.

Nadia looked around. Chloe was right. The Bridget Mason students scattered throughout the bleachers were almost all from the school's different sports teams. Not a Dungeons & Dragons Club member or a mathlete in sight. Nadia didn't see any other nerds, or artsy kids, or goth kids, or even pastel-goth kids. Just sporty kids as far as the eye could see.

As if on cue, two eighth graders wearing volleyball sweatshirts pushed their way into their row, practically stepping on Vikram's nachos.

"Um, do you mind?" Nadia said.

"Yeah, I *do* mind," one of the girls said. She was tall, with long, straight jet-black hair that Nadia would have admired if she wasn't so annoyed. "You're in our seats."

Sarah jumped up. "We'll move!" She scooted down the row, pulling the rest of the Nerd Patrol along with her.

"Well, that was rude," Nadia said. "There's plenty of room."

"Eh," Sarah said. "I kinda get it. I'd be annoyed if a random kid sat in my favorite seat at a debate tournament." She shrugged. "We *are* sort of in their territory."

"But this is the gym," Nadia said. "The sports kids don't own it."

Adam shifted in his seat. "Whatever. I didn't mind the excuse to stand up. I never realized how uncomfortable these bleachers are. My ttub hurts."

Nadia frowned. "Are you talking backward again?"

About a month ago, Adam, who loved all things tech related, had discovered how to play audio backward and now peppered his commentary with backward words that

7

everyone had to decipher. It was both endearing and slightly annoying.

"*Sey*," he said with a grin. Then he pointed to the court, narrating the action like a sports announcer. "Jason gets the pass and immediately goes into a triple threat position. He sizes up his opponent . . . does a pump fake . . . and pulls up for the jump shot. SWISH!" He turned to Nadia, a teasing grin on his face. "That was us. You can clap now."

Nadia applauded politely. She was amused to discover that even on the basketball court, Jason paused for a moment to toss his shaggy sandy-blond hair out of his blue eyes. The Nerd Patrol's newest member brought his own brand of nerdery to the group—endless knowledge of plays, stats, and strategies. His sports brain was a new—and welcome— point of view. Nadia looked over at Sarah, who tried to push her new cat-eye glasses up on her face, forgetting that she was wearing a huge GO, BRIDGET MASON! foam hand. She ended up poking herself in the nose. Nadia giggled.

Yes, the Nerd Patrol were definitely expanding their horizons, thanks to Jason.

The ref blew a whistle and the teams went back to their benches.

"What are they doing now?" Nadia asked Adam.

"Tenth Street Middle is taking a time-out," he explained.

Their mascot, a huge green shell on its back, began moving around the court super slowly. The Tenth Street fans seemed to think this was hysterical.

"Tenth Street's mascot is a *terrapin*?" Nadia asked.

8

Adam gave her a look. "It is," he said. "But how did you know that? Most people assume it's just a turtle."

Nadia felt an excited buzz start up in her brain, like she always did when she sensed an opportunity to share interesting facts. "Well, its shell has a pattern," she said. "Also, it has red stripes on each side of its head, which leads me to believe that it's a red-eared slider terrapin." She laughed. "I just didn't think mascots were that . . . specific."

Nadia was distracted from the terrapin when the Bridget Mason cheerleaders started a cheer:

"Hey, hey you, get out of our way

Today is the day we will blow you away!"

Sarah looked over at Nadia. "Eh," they said in unison. It was pretty uninspiring, as far as cheers went.

As the time-out clock buzzed, the teams ran back out on the court.

"Let's go, Bridget Mason!" Adam shouted. Then he turned to Nadia and said, "We really could win this."

The Tenth Street cheerleaders started a routine:

"Extra, extra, read all about it:

Your mascot is boring and there's no doubt about it!

When you're up, you're up! When you're down, you're down!

When you're Bridget Mason Middle, you're going down!"

The cheerleaders ended their cheer pointing to the far corner of the gym. Nadia followed their gaze.

"Is that—" She nudged Vikram. "The Bridget Mason Petunia?"

"What else could it be?" Vikram said, shaking his head.

Nadia sighed, staring at the kid in costume. He was dressed in a green spandex onesie, a large headpiece surrounding his face with pink petals. He was just kind of standing there sticking his leafy arms out, acting like, well, a flower.

Nadia wasn't surprised she hadn't noticed the mascot until now. She was halfway through fifth grade before she realized that Bridget Mason even *had* a mascot.

The terrapin pointed to the petunia and laughed. Then it

fell onto its back and pretended it was stuck. It waved its arms and legs helplessly. The Tenth Street fans roared with laughter.

"I heard that poor kid didn't even want to be the petunia," Vikram said. "He tried out for the basketball team and didn't make it. Coach Zuckerman hadn't had any applicants for the mascot, so he said the kid could come to basketball practices if he agreed to be the mascot at games."

Nadia watched as the petunia sighed and walked closer to the Bridget Mason cheerleaders. There, he struck a slightly more enthusiastic flower pose.

"Way to photosynthesize!" a boy wearing a Tenth Street sweatshirt shouted mockingly.

For the rest of the game, Nadia watched the mascots instead of the players. The terrapin was *way* more entertaining than the petunia. Where the turtle danced and shook its shell to the music, the petunia swayed back and forth like a blossom in the breeze. Yawn.

As the game went on, the cheerleaders' insults continued.

"Your mascot is so boring! We'll just keep on scoring!"

And Tenth Street did. They won 55 to 22.

"Well, that was *lufwa*," said Adam after the game as the friends waited for Jason by the fountain at the Bridget Mason school entrance.

It took a minute for the rest of the Nerd Patrol to decipher the word.

"Yeah," Chloe finally said. "Super awful."

"I think all the mascot mocking had a lot to do with us losing," Nadia said "A petunia is so . . . wilty. A terrapin is a little strange, but at least there's potential for it to be entertaining. Doesn't it bother you all? They were mocking us the whole game."

"Eh, that's part of sports," said Adam. "Fans make fun of each other."

Sarah shrugged.

Nadia shook her head. "But we're handing it to them on a silver platter. Shouldn't we do something about it?"

"My big brother tried to get it changed a bunch of years ago," said Chloe. "But Principal Taylor refused. They say he actually used to *be* the petunia and that he still keeps his old costume somewhere in his office."

Now that did not surprise Nadia one bit. Their principal loved Bridget Mason Middle School—and its students—like nobody's business. And he wasn't afraid to show it. Like last semester, when he started DJing at school events. He himself had graduated from Bridget Mason Middle way back in the stone ages—the 1980s. If you looked at his yearbook (and she had) you could see Zachary Taylor in all his mulleted glory, his extremely long list of extracurriculars taking up two columns underneath his photo.

The door of the gym pushed open and Jason appeared. He looked pretty disappointed.

"Thanks for coming," he said. "Sorry we lost so bad."

"Are you kidding me?" said Nadia. "It was awesome! And you made four goals, too!"

Jason laughed. "Oh, Nadia, you crack me up," he said. "But geez, that was a tough game."

Two of Jason's teammates came outside, their duffel bags slung over their shoulders. "Yo, Flanagan, wanna bounce?" one of them called out.

"I'll see you guys later," said Jason. "I'm gonna hang out with these peeps."

The two boys looked surprised. "Suit yourself," one of them said with a shrug.

When they were out of earshot, Nadia nudged Jason. "So, how does it feel to be a spy?"

"Huh?" Jason said.

Nadia had been thinking about this ever since those eighth graders made them move seats. "It's like there are two schools—or more—in our one school," she said. "The Nerd School and the Jock School, and probably the Art School, and the Goth Schools, and other ones I don't even know about. And we don't overlap much." The rest of the Nerd Patrol was listening now. "We're a school divided. But you"—she pointed to Jason—"you're a crossover. Kind of like a spy."

Jason laughed. "I guess I am the exception."

Adam put an arm around Jason. "How about some ice cream for this *exceptional* friend? My treat." He quickly looked around at the others. "Well, just Jason," he said. "My allowance isn't that big!"

When Nadia got home from Ice Scream that afternoon (a double-scoop cone of peanut-butter-and-chocolate and blueberry pie seemed to cheer Jason right up), she was still thinking about the way their school was so divided. It wasn't so much that the groups were at odds. It was just sad that they were so separate. Imagine how awesome it would be if the sports kids showed up to support the mathletes, and vice versa. Maybe the petunia stuff wouldn't have bothered the team so much today if they'd had bleachers full of Bridget Mason students there to drown out the Terrapin cheerleaders.

All of a sudden, Nadia got an idea. She opened up her laptop and started an email:

TO: Taylor, Principal Zachary
FROM: Youssef, Nadia
RE: Bridget Mason Mascot

Dear Principal Taylor,
I would like to make a suggestion. It concerns our school mascot. No one seems to like it and we are being mocked by the other sports teams. It seems as if it might be time to pick a new one, a mascot that represents all our students. I know this may be a sensitive issue, so I hope you will give this careful consideration.
Sincerely,
Nadia Youssef

She knew it was a long shot, what with Taylor's history as the petunia, but even if Chloe's brother had asked about it years ago, it wouldn't hurt for her to ask again. And maybe it would give all the students something to work on together.

Nadia read her email through one more time, then pressed send. She had nothing to lose, right?

Chapter Two

Early Monday morning, Nadia stopped to look in the mirror before heading down to breakfast. She smiled, admiring her two-toned denim skirt and her Isis T-shirt under an oversized cardigan. Her brand-new combat boots and her ancient Egyptian, hippopotamus-shaped amulet necklace completed her first-day-back-to-school-after-the-holiday-break outfit. (She never went anywhere without her amulet, especially after she'd lost it last month. That had not been a good week.) She turned to the bobbleheads on her bookshelf and addressed one of the seventy-nine she owned.

"What do you think?" she asked journalist Nellie Bly, a holiday gift from Adam. "Is this a good outfit for the first day of the sixth-grade newspaper?"

Nellie just stared at her.

"There are five sixth-grade classes, so every two months a different class gets to run the school newspaper," Nadia explained. "Now it's my class's turn. I get to be a real journalist, just like you! Have any tips for me?"

Nellie continued to stare.

"Well, I'm sure I'll figure it out," Nadia said confidently. She stole another glance at herself and spotted the Graceland postcard stuck into the corner of her mirror. She sighed, thinking of Titi.

From the moment she had placed her hand on the amulet she bought at a Cairo bazaar last summer and accidentally said the magic word *help*, her life had changed completely. That action had released Titi, an ancient Egyptian teacher who had been trapped inside the amulet for thousands of years. After getting over the initial shock and disbelief, they began to discover how the spell worked. At first, Titi could only appear on paper—notebooks, posters, books, magazines, and more—sort of like an animated doodle.

After some trial—and a significant amount of error—Nadia and Titi realized that, in order for him to resume his fully human form, he needed to help Nadia solve seven problems. With each solution, he received a new power.

Before Titi helped Nadia with a seventh solution, Nadia

brought Adam in on the secret. He was still the only member of the Nerd Patrol who knew Titi existed.

Titi's seventh and last solution, the one that freed him from his paper prison, involved Jason. When Jason had first come to Bridget Mason, he'd been a total jerk, making fun of Nadia's Egyptian heritage and cracking all sorts of other offensive jokes. But the former bully was becoming a good friend, thanks to Titi's help.

After all that craziness last fall, it had been a bit of a relief when Titi became human and ran off to Graceland. Things went back to normal for Nadia, but she missed him popping up in her notebooks when she least expected it.

And now it had been several months since Titi left for Graceland. He'd sent her several postcards in the first few weeks, but she hadn't heard from him since that last postcard back in October. She wondered if he'd forgotten her already.

"Yalla habibti!" called her mother. "Hurry up, my dear!"

"Coming, Mama!" Nadia yelled back. She grabbed her backpack and headed downstairs.

"Good morning," said her father from the kitchen table, putting down his coffee mug. "The early bird catches the perm."

"What's a perm?" Nadia asked.

Baba laughed. "Clearly you didn't grow up in the eighties."

Nadia chuckled at Baba. When they'd first arrived in the United States from Egypt when she was six years old, her father often unintentionally mixed up American expressions. Now, almost six years later, his English was nearly perfect and he deliberately mangled expressions to make her laugh.

"Ta-da," said Mama, placing breakfast on the table. "I made taameya for the first day back to school."

"Mmmmm," said Nadia appreciatively. Taameya was a super-tasty falafel-on-steroids dish and one of her favorite breakfasts. Her mother must have gotten up extra early to prepare it. "Thanks, Mama," she said, standing up to kiss her on the cheek.

After Nadia finished up her taameya, she grabbed her backpack.

"Salaam," she said as she headed out the door. "Goodbye, Mama and Baba. Have a good day at work." Her parents were both surgeons and worked at the same hospital. They'd met in medical school back in Cairo, where they had both grown up.

"Good luck on your first day back," called Mama.

"Break a rib," added Baba with a grin.

Nadia was eager to get to school and was glad to see Adam already waiting for her at the corner.

He fell into step next to her.

"You ready for the first day back?" he asked.

"I am! And you'll never believe it, I actually emailed Taylor about changing the mascot," she said.

"Impressive," said Adam. "But pointless, I bet."

After going to their lockers, Nadia and Adam headed to homeroom. She waved to Jason and Sarah before she sat down.

"Welcome back from the holiday break, class," their teacher Ms. Arena said. "I trust that you all got plenty of rest and relaxation and are ready to hit the ground running this semester."

There was a terrible screech over the loudspeaker and everyone jumped.

"This is your principal, Mr. Zachary Taylor, reporting for duty. Good morning, students. I hope you all had a totally awesome break. I used the time off to really throw myself into my clogging lessons. And I'm pleased to announce that I've finally mastered the scuff up! Though, truth be told, my downstairs neighbors were not quite as thrilled about my accomplishment as I was."

Nadia laughed. She'd missed Principal Taylor's goofiness over the break.

"So I have an announcement to make," the principal continued. "Unfortunately, something came up for our beloved sixth-grade social studies teacher, Mr. Decker, over the holidays and he informed me he would be unable to continue teaching this semester."

Nadia turned to Adam and made a frowny face. Mr. Decker was one of her favorite teachers, not only because he was good at his job but because he saw her Egyptian background as something fascinating, something that made her interesting instead of weird.

"Fortunately," Principal Taylor continued, "I was able to find a new teacher to join us on short notice. His name is Mr. Ferrari, and while he has some big shoes to fill, I'm sure you'll give him a big Bridget Mason welcome!

"And we have one other new member on our staff: Mr. Flores, our janitor. Please be sure to say hello when you see him in the hallways. Now, on to some other announcements: I wish the eighth graders well as they start to brainstorm their community outreach project. And similar well wishes to class 605, who will run the sixth-grade newspaper for the next two months. We look forward to your first issue! And finally, I'm sure you know that we have a big basketball game coming up against our rivals, Westside Middle, next month. This is just a heads-up that DJ Ed U. Cator plans to make an appearance at halftime to really jazz things up!"

Jason stood up and fluttered his fingers. "Jazz hands!" he said. This made everyone, even Ms. Arena, laugh.

"Now keep on truckin', kids," the principal concluded. "This is Principal Taylor, over and out."

Chapter Three

Nadia glanced down at her class schedule to double-check that she had language arts first period. Bridget Mason had rotating schedules, which meant her classes were at different times each day. She headed to class, a little skip in her step.

When the last student was settled in their seat, Ms. Tovey shut the door. She turned to the class, her cheeks flushed. Nadia realized that her teacher was just as excited about their class getting their turn at the paper as she was.

"The time has come!" Ms. Tovey announced. "It's your turn to create and publish our school's biweekly newspaper. And learn about journalism in the process!"

Nadia's hand shot up.

"Yes, Nadia?" said her teacher.

"Does someone get to be editor in chief? I'd like to volunteer for that position," she said.

Ms. Tovey laughed. "I appreciate your enthusiasm, but that's my job as your teacher," she said. "Now, as I was saying, it will be your job to present news and important information to your classmates clearly and concisely. And you must do it in a trustworthy, truthful, and unbiased way. But first," she continued. "Each sixth-grade class gets to pick the content of the paper, and name it, too."

Nadia recalled last year, when one sixth-grade class called the paper the *Mason Manga* and all the stories were told in comics. It was very creative, but Nadia was hoping for a more traditional approach.

"So our goals today are to choose our approach to the paper and a name. And then we'll also decide what everyone's roles will be."

A girl named Emma raised her hand. "I like the classic approach," she said. "Stories on school news with photographs."

Nadia smiled. A girl after her own heart.

"Yes, our paper will report on school news," the teacher said. "But it can be so much more, if we want it to be. Will we also write about current events and how they affect our school? Will we run editorials stating our opinions? Will we have cartoons, horoscopes, puzzles, other fun features? The choice is up to you!"

"I think it should have serious content," said Nadia.

"It's more important to be informed than to be entertained."

"I agree," said a boy named Mateo.

Oona raised her hand. Oona wasn't part of the Nerd Patrol but Nadia sometimes hung out with her. Nadia noticed that she had dyed her hair purple over the break. It looked really pretty and Nadia made a mental note to tell her. "I don't know," Oona said. "Can't we do both? So there's something for everyone?"

After a lot of back and forth among the students, they decided that Oona was right, the paper should be a mix—serious articles about important issues as well as short, snappy ones and some fun content, too. Mateo, who was considered the best artist in the sixth grade, offered to draw cartoons. Adam suggested that one story in each issue could have a link to a video component, with extra information not found in the article. Ms. Tovey scribbled the ideas on the whiteboard, then stepped back. "Now how about we throw some suggestions around for our newspaper's name?"

The ideas started coming. The *Mason Messenger*. The *Middle School Ages*. *Notes from School*. The *Bridget Mason Times*.

"The *Daily Dose!*" someone shouted out.

Nadia made an "are you kidding me?" face. "News flash!" she said. "The paper comes out every two weeks, not every day, remember?" She didn't mean to sound obnoxious. But really!

"*Newsflash!*" said Abby. "That should be our name!"

Nadia shook her head. "Oh, no, that's not what I—"

NEWSFLASH, Ms. Tovey wrote on the board. "I love it!"

Nadia shrugged and smiled. She was totally a natural at this whole journalism thing.

"The first issue of Newsflash will debut in just over a week, so let's figure out who will do what," Ms. Tovey continued. "Who wants to write for the paper?"

Several hands shot up, Nadia's included.

"Awesome," Ms. Tovey said. "As we discussed, we'll have both hard and soft news. The hard news will be news articles and the soft news could be pieces on entertainment or maybe even an advice column. We can also have editorials, which reflect the opinions of the newspaper, and columns, which reflect the opinions of the writer."

Nadia's face lit up. She knew a lot of facts and had a lot of opinions. This would be a big audience to share them with! Her hand shot up again. "Could I write a column for our first edition?"

Ms. Tovey nodded. "That sounds great, Nadia."

As her teacher began writing down everyone's assignments, Nadia grinned. She was going to write a column! Nellie Bly would be so proud. And she knew exactly what she was going to call it: As a Matter of Fact, by Nadia Youssef. Now she just had to figure out what to write about.

After she left language arts, Nadia felt like she was floating on a cloud. It lasted almost the whole day. But as she approached her social studies classroom—her last class that day—her spirits sank. Students had been raving about Mr. Ferrari all day long, but she knew that things weren't going to be the same without Mr. Decker.

She opened the classroom door. *Time to see what this new teacher is all about.*

"Whoa," she said.

The classroom walls were covered in mosaic murals. Tall columns that looked remarkably like marble stood in each corner. There were several statues placed throughout the room. The new teacher had even painted the classroom ceiling deep blue and added twinkling lights for stars. Nadia reached out and lightly knocked on a nearby column, expecting to hear the hollow sound of papier-mâché. But the column was solid. Its surface was even cool to the touch, just like real marble. How had the new teacher pulled that off?

The students settled into their seats, looking around in awe as they waited for Mr. Ferrari. The bell rang, but still no teacher.

All of a sudden there was a *boom!* from the front of the room, followed by a cloud of blue smoke. Nadia coughed.

As the smoke began to clear, Nadia could make out a figure. The new teacher was wearing a mask, a wreath of leaves on his head, a toga, and a pair of sandals. He stood stiffly, like a statue. The class stared in stunned silence.

Adam, who sat in the next row, turned around in his seat. "What the heck is going on?" he mouthed to Nadia.

Nadia shrugged, returning her eyes to the toga'd teacher.

The man sprang to life. "What! No applause?" He threw his arms into the air. "Didn't like my grand entrance? I practiced all morning. I'm crushed!"

25

No answer. Oona coughed, waving the remnants of hazy smoke away from her face.

The teacher took a deep bow. "Allow me to introduce myself. My name is Mr. Ferrari and I'm your new teacher. My job this semester is to teach you just how magical history can be!"

Nadia stared. Could it be?

"Where's Mr. Decker?" a boy named Mark asked. "Why'd he leave?"

Mr. Ferrari shrugged. "Beats me. Family emergency? Sabbatical? A winning streak on *Family Feud*?" He took a breath. "Whatever it is, he's not here and I am! Don't worry, my teaching credentials are impeccable. I have a huge amount of experience. In fact, you could say that I've been a teacher for practically three millennia! But I promise not to rest on my laurels!"

Nadia let out a bark of a laugh. This was unbelievable.

"So can anyone guess which ancient civilization we'll be learning about this semester?" Mr. Ferrari asked.

"Um, ancient Greece?" asked a girl named Maddie.

Mr. Ferrari gasped, his hands on his hips. "Do I look like Pericles to you?" He shook his head in disbelief and put his hands on either side of his mouth like a megaphone. "Paging Julius Caesar!" He dropped his hands down to his sides and became another character.

"Yes, was someone looking for me?" he said in a deep voice. "Does anyone know what my last words were?" He looked around the classroom. "Give up? 'Make sure they name a salad after me!'" Not even pausing for a laugh, he pointed to his outfit. "And this is unmistakably a toga, worn only by Roman citizens." He leaned toward Maddie. "You didn't . . . you didn't think that this was a himation, did you?"

"Um . . . no?" said Maddie.

"Because that's Greek to me!" Mr. Ferrari cracked himself up so much he had to lean against one of the columns to catch his breath.

He pointed to it. "And I don't need to tell any of you what kind of column this is, amirite? As I'm sure you all already know, the Romans were suckers for a nice Corinthian."

He walked back over to Maddie's desk. "Don't mind me," he told her. "Greece was actually a fine guess."

Maddie looked super confused. "Okay, thanks?" she said.

With a whoop, Mr. Ferrari made a flying leap toward the next row of desks. "Friends, Romans, students, lend me your ears!" he cried. He reached down and seemed to pull two gigantic fake ears out of thin air from the sides of Andrew's head.

That broke the spell of confusion that had been hanging over the classroom. The students roared with laughter. The next thing Nadia knew, Mr. Ferrari was handing out buckets of popcorn to the students. Now where had those come from?

He whipped off his mask, giving Nadia a big wink. "Enjoy the show!" he cried.

Nadia gasped as the rest of the class cheered. It *was* him!

As Mr. Ferrari began to lecture about the founding of Rome and the story of Romulus and Remus, Adam turned

to Nadia, his mouth open in shock. Neither of them could sit still the rest of class.

The end-of-class bell rang. Usually, the students jumped out of their seats, eager to go home for the day. But nobody moved a muscle, not wanting to take their eyes off Mr. Ferrari.

The teacher laughed and took a deep bow. "Class dismissed!" he said. He waved goodbye as the students reluctantly filed out of the classroom. "Oh, Nadia and Adam, would you mind staying back for a moment?"

Nadia smiled. "Sure."

Adam nodded.

After the last student left, Mr. Ferrari turned to the two friends.

"For the love of Tutankhamen!" he cried. "Get up here and greet your long-lost friend properly!"

Chapter Four

"**T**itiiiiii!!!" Nadia and Adam shouted in unison. They gave him a big hug.

"Suffering scarabs!" Titi said when they pulled away. "The band is back together!" He grinned. "Don't get me wrong, Memphis was amazing. Well, except for the time that chandelier fell on my head at Graceland. True story. But anyway, when I got your postcard last month, Nadia, I was on the first plane back."

"My postcard?" said Nadia at the same time that Adam said, "A chandelier fell on your head?"

"Crashed right on top of my melon," said Titi, patting his bald head. "The tourists were traumatized. But believe it or not, I didn't get a scratch on me. It seems old Titi is immortal—must be a side effect of the hippo magic. Not that I'm complaining!"

He sat down at his desk. "So how was my first lesson?" he asked eagerly. "I hope it wasn't too boring!"

Nadia laughed. "Are you kidding? It was amazing!"

Titi stood and began to joyfully spin in a circle. "It feels so amazing to have students again. Oh, how I've missed it!" He stopped, looking a bit dizzy.

Nadia laughed. "Well, we've missed *you*, Titi. You're going to make an amazing social studies teacher. I learned so much from you last fall—"

"Yeah," Adam said. "If it weren't for you, I wouldn't know how to do this." He launched into an air guitar solo worthy of Elvis Presley. "It definitely got me some attention at the winter dance."

"You sure that was the right kind of attention, my man?" Titi teased. "But yes! Whatever you two need, I'm here for you. Homework help, life stuff. My door is always open. You're Mr. Ferrari's original—and favorite—students, you know."

Nadia smirked at Titi. "Mr. Ferrari, huh? What's up with that name?"

Titi nodded, looking pleased with himself. "I just picked the coolest, most American-sounding name I could think of."

Nadia laughed. "Did you know that a Ferrari is an *Italian* sports car?"

"Huh," Titi said. "I did not. But oscillating obelisks, Nadia—I've missed those fun facts of yours!" He swung around a marble column. "Now, no offense to Mr. Decker,

30

who I'm sure was a super-cool dude, but social studies is going to ROCK this semester!"

And then all three of them launched into the greatest air guitar trio that Bridget Mason Middle School had ever seen.

After dinner that night, Nadia checked her email. Principal Taylor had written back! She held her breath as she read his reply:

> TO: Youssef, Nadia
> FROM: Taylor, Principal Zachary
> RE: RE: Bridget Mason Middle Mascot
>
> Dear Nadia,
> I'm always tickled when students show their school spirit. A new mascot is a wonderful idea! I'll take it from here—you can expect an announcement tomorrow. Thanks for bringing it up!
>
> Sincerely,
> Principal Taylor

"See?" Nadia said to her Alexander Hamilton bobble-head. "It never hurts to speak up." She laughed. "Not that I need to tell *you* that!"

The magician plopped down on his bed. He was exhausted. Plan Number Three was working well, or now it was, at least. It had gotten off to a rocky start.

Plan Number One had been the chandelier. That obviously failed. So the magician had decided that if he couldn't off his old nemesis, the only way to get rid of him would be to somehow get him back inside the hippo amulet and then destroy it. For Plan Number Two, he'd swiped the amulet from the girl, then made his way back to Tennessee with it. He attended one of the teacher's ridiculous Elvis shows at the Hunka Hunka Burning Love Karaoke Lounge. Then during a raucous round of applause, he tried to send the teacher into the amulet with the same spell he'd used three thousand years ago. But the teacher remained up onstage, rhinestones shimmering as bright as ever.

The whole thing was extremely disappointing.

The magician had gone back to his hotel and raided the nuts again while he thought things through. He had been afraid this would be the case—that he wouldn't have the power to send the teacher back. It meant he'd have to involve the girl. But it made sense when he thought about it. If she was the one who had freed the teacher, then she was the only one who could send him back.

Of course, the girl and the teacher would need to be in the same place to do that. Khefren figured it was easier to get the teacher to California than to get the girl to Tennessee. He couldn't believe his luck when he found out that a teaching position had opened up at the school. It had taken only one forged postcard to get the teacher to apply for the position.

His next decision—Plan Number Three—hadn't been easy. Oh, how he hated the thought of taking over another human's body! It was even worse than shape-shifting into a rodent! But he couldn't exactly waltz up to the girl as himself and demand that she send the teacher back, now could he? She'd refuse and the teacher would be onto him. So he picked someone with access to the school and took over their body.

He sighed and grabbed another bag of mixed nuts. His cravings were waning a bit, but he was still eating three to five bags a day.

Now that he had taken over this body, he was in close proximity to the girl and the teacher every day.

He had them right where he wanted them. He'd have to be careful that the girl didn't send both of them back to the amulet, but he already had an idea for that. Names were a powerful thing, and she didn't even know what his was. In fact, she didn't even know he still existed.

Chapter Five

What are you going to write your first column about, habibti?" Baba asked at breakfast on Thursday morning.

"Not sure yet," Nadia said. "But our content isn't due until Monday, so I have some time."

"Well, I'm sure you'll figure it out," Baba said encouragingly. "You know what they say, genius is ten percent inspiration and ninety percent *respiration*."

Nadia gave him a sly grin. "Sounds like I should start taking more deep breaths. See you later, Baba!"

"Hey, Nadia!" Jason said when she joined him in the lunch line later that day. "What's super cool and isn't pink?"

Nadia frowned. Jason's jokes often made her think, but this setup seemed a little odd.

"Give up?"' Jason said. "Any mascot that's NOT the petunia!"

Nadia chuckled. "I'm glad you're excited that we might get a new mascot."

Principal Taylor had announced the mascot contest on Tuesday, and it was all anyone had been talking about since. The contest was already giving the students something in common!

This was the plan: Students had until tomorrow to submit their mascot nominations. The Art Club would create posters for each nominee over the weekend and display them on the bulletin board outside the main office on Monday. Students would then have until Wednesday at lunchtime to vote for their favorite, narrowing the mascots down to two finalists. Then students would have two weeks to build school spirit for the mascot they supported. And finally, they would vote in a final election. The winning mascot would be announced at a special spirit rally, in time for the big game against Westside Middle.

When Nadia got up to the lunch counter, she smiled at her favorite lunch lady.

"Hey, Mrs. Farley," Nadia said. "I'll have chicken nuggets and fries, please."

Mrs. Farley added extra fries to the order, like she always did. "Here you go!" she said with a wink. "How's it going? Hey, do you have that new social studies teacher? I hear he's a real laugh riot."

"He's pretty entertaining," said Nadia. "Thanks, Mrs. Farley!"

Nadia and the rest of the group headed to their lunch table. Nadia sat down next to Sarah, who had brought her own lunch: rice and kimchee. Sarah sometimes brought traditional Korean food for lunch, just as Nadia sometimes brought Egyptian food like besarah or koushary.

"So," Jason said. "You nerds always have awesome ideas. Who's nominating something?"

"I think our mascot should be a bumblebee," offered Chloe. "They're productive and also a little bit dangerous. Plus, the costume could be super cute. Maybe the wings could really flap!"

That buzz started up in Nadia's brain. "Did you know bumblebees flap their wings back and forth, not up and down?"

"We could make that happen on a costume," Vikram said. "It would be super fly." He paused so everyone could roll their eyes at his pun.

"A bumblebee?" Jason said. "Isn't that a little . . . tiny? I was thinking more like a cougar." He held his hands up like claws. "Something to really scare our opponents. Make them shudder every time they see the mascot on our jerseys!"

"Um, hello," Vikram said. "A mascot's role is not to intimidate. It's to entertain. We need something funny!"

"I know!" Adam said, eyeing Nadia's chicken nuggets. "What about a food?"

"You're always hungry, aren't you?" Sarah teased Adam. He made a face at her and pressed on. "It would be unexpected. I can see it now. The Bridget Mason . . . Gherkin Pickles! Or the Wiener Schnitzels!"

Nadia had to smile. Adam was embracing his newly found Austrian roots, apparently mainly through food.

"Well, I don't think the mascot's main role is to intimidate or to entertain," Sarah said. "It's to represent us to the community. To tell everyone who we are, whether that's at a sports game or mathlete tournament, or just on a T-shirt someone randomly wears on a Saturday at the park. Do you really want a pickle to be the face of Bridget Mason?"

"The Bridget Mason Pickle-Faces," Adam said. "I think I actually could get on board with that."

Nadia chuckled, but her friends had some really good points. If the mascot was going to unify the school, they had to find one that somehow felt like it represented everyone, and also somehow fulfilled all those purposes. Did an animal—or anything—like that even exist?

Nadia pushed her chicken nuggets aside, an idea forming in her head. "What if the mascot was a mythological creature? Something cool and different that does a lot of those things or even is many things? Something more unique than a bear or a wolf . . . or even a pickle?"

"You mean like Sheshnaag?" Vikram said.

Nadia leaned forward. "What's that?"

"It's from Indian mythology," he explained. "A serpent with a hundred heads."

"Whoa," Nadia said. "The costume could be tricky. But yeah, something more creative like that, you know?"

She gobbled down the rest of her nuggets. Vikram's suggestion had given her yet another idea.

"Hey, Adam," she said, "I forgot my pencil case in my locker." This was their code for Let's go see Titi. They had come up with it during the walk to school yesterday, and Nadia was pleased to have the opportunity to use it.

"Bummer," said Adam. "Do you want to borrow a pen—"

Nadia glared at him until he realized what she was saying.

"Oh, I mean, I'll go with you," Adam said. "See you all later."

They found Titi sitting cross-legged on his desk in a gladiator costume. His eyes were closed and his arms rested on his knees, his thumbs and index fingers touching.

"What's he doing?" Adam whispered to Nadia.

"Meditating," Titi said, his eyes still closed.

Adam backed up. "Oh, I'm so sorry to disturb you."

Titi snapped his eyes open. "It's all fine, pal o' mine," he said. "I was just finishing up. I'm telling you, there is nothing that makes me want to meditate more than interacting with middle school students. The drama! The eye rolling! Sometimes I feel like I need a full suit of armor just to deflect all the sass."

"Is that what the outfit is for?" Nadia asked.

"Nope," Titi said, climbing off the desk with a clang. "I'm getting into character; we're starting a unit on the Colosseum today. Hey—speaking of characters, what's the latest buzz about the mascot? I can just imagine the costumes."

38

"I knew you'd be into that!" said Nadia. "I want to nominate something. Maybe a mythological creature, but I'm not sure where to start. That's where you come in."

"Can you still do comic book dives?" Adam asked, opening his backpack and pulling out the Egyptian comic that Nadia had given him last summer. She had picked it up at the same flea market where she had gotten the amulet. She and Titi discovered that he had the power to dive inside it to any point in history and bring Nadia and Adam along. They'd done several dives into ancient Egyptian history when he was first released from the amulet, and then some more into other parts of history when Nadia brought Adam in on the secret. That's how Adam had discovered his background.

"Snefru's loincloth! It's nice to see this old thing again!" Titi said, picking up the comic. "I'm pretty sure I can still do dives. You may not have noticed, but since I became human, my magic is even better than it was on paper. Feats of skill and strength, outfit changes, making things appear and disappear, and I can still do this of course!" Titi snapped his fingers and—POOF!—suddenly appeared on a poster of Pompeii next to the whiteboard, a tiny animated version of himself. Then he jumped to a calendar over his desk, then to a list of upcoming cafeteria specials. "Paper hopping is still one of the great joys of my life! Let's give the comic book dive a try!" POOF! He was human Titi again.

"So, where to?" he continued. "The fall of the Berlin Wall? The Gettysburg Address? The height of the Aztec Empire?" He pointed a thumb over his shoulder at the

Pompeii poster. "The eruption of Vesuvius? From a safe distance, of course." His eyes brightened. "Ooh! What about one of the royal weddings? Maybe one of King Henry the Eighth's? He had a few, if I recall correctly!"

"Focus, Titi!" Nadia said. "I'm interested in mythological creatures, remember?"

"Gotcha," Titi said. He nodded. "I've got a few ideas. Ready?"

WHOOSH!

Nadia felt a blast of wind and was suddenly falling, falling, falling. Finally . . .

Oof. She landed in front of a large building with Adam and Titi next to her.

THAT DRAGON WAS COOL.

DON'T YOU MEAN HOT, NADIA? DRAGONS BREATHE FIRE.

WRONG, SIR! NOT CHINESE DRAGONS!

NOW, THIS CREATURE IS THE CUERO FROM CHILE.

EEK!

Cuero (Chile)
- Bloodsucking mouth
- Hooked claws
- Sometimes has many eyes

NEXT WE HAVE THE ZHAR-PTITSA, OR FIREBIRD, FROM RUSSIA.

IT'S BEEN KNOWN TO STEAL FROM THE RICH AND GIVE TO THE POOR

AWW, LIKE AN AVIAN ROBIN HOOD!

IT'S SO PRETTY!

Zhar-Ptitsa (Russia)
- Glowing golden feathers
- Crystal eyes

Nadia blinked. They were back in Titi's classroom. "That was incredible," she said, her eyes gleaming. She had really missed those comic book dives!

"Thank you, thank you very much," said Titi, doing his very best Elvis Presley impression.

"So, Nadia, tell us. You're going with El Cuero, right?" joked Adam.

"As much as I'd love to see that costume, it's not gonna happen," Nadia said. "I'm pretty sure I know which one I'm going to nominate, but I'm keeping it to myself for now. I need to do more research."

"Awwwww! That's no fun!" Adam whined.

"Building anticipation for a big reveal," Titi said. "I like your style."

Nadia grinned at him. Having Titi back was even better than she had thought it would be. She made a mental note to ask to do more comic book dives. Those were seriously fun!

When she got home that afternoon, Nadia did some research about her mascot of choice. The more she read, the better the mascot got.

She printed out the nomination form and filled it out. She tucked it into her backpack so she could turn it in tomorrow.

Then she opened a new document and started typing away. Thanks to her conversation with the Nerd Patrol, she not only knew what she'd nominate for a mascot, but also exactly what she'd write for her newspaper column. Before she knew it, she'd finished. She sent it off to Ms. Tovey.

"Four whole days before the deadline," she said to Nellie Bly. "You better move over. There's a new reporter on the scene."

Chapter Six

Monday morning, as they stood waiting on the corner for the crossing guard, Nadia turned to Adam. "T-minus twenty-four hours until the first issue of *Newsflash* comes out," she said. They'd be receiving their copies in homeroom the next day. "I can't wait to see my—I mean our—names in print!"

"Totally," Adam said. "And the mascot posters will be up when we get to school. Did I tell you I submitted an idea?"

"Was it a pickle?" asked Nadia.

"Nope," Adam said, smiling mysteriously. "You'll see soon enough."

As they approached the school, Nadia's pulse quickened. She speed-walked to the main hallway, where she found a group of kids clustered in front of the bulletin board.

Nadia stood on her tiptoes to see the posters of the candidates.

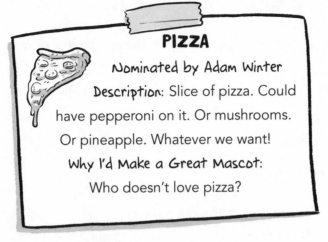

PIZZA

Nominated by Adam Winter

Description: Slice of pizza. Could have pepperoni on it. Or mushrooms. Or pineapple. Whatever we want!

Why I'd Make a Great Mascot:
Who doesn't love pizza?

Nadia rolled her eyes. Everyone did love pizza. But did that mean it would make a good mascot?

HAWK

Nominated by Mia Catacutan

Description: Powerful bird of prey

Why I'd Make a Great Mascot:
I am strong, impressive, and fast. I would inspire our students to spread their wings and fly, and intimidate other schools with my hawk-eyed stare.

"Hawk-eyed stare," a girl in a cheerleader uniform said to someone behind Nadia. "Nice, Mia."

Nadia glanced over her shoulder. It was one of the volleyball girls from the bleachers at the basketball game!

A hawk's not bad, Nadia thought. *A little unoriginal, but a solid choice.* She liked the "spread their wings and fly" part;

47

she kind of wished she'd used it in her own description.

Nadia scanned the other mascot entries: a knight, a Boston terrier, Jason's cougar, Chloe's bumblebee, a hummingbird, a gecko, a rhinoceros, and a woodchuck. Then finally, she came to her own entry:

SPHINX

Nominated by Nadia Youssef

Description: An ancient creature with the head of a human, the body of a lion, and sometimes eagle wings and a serpent's tail. The symbol of royalty and protection in ancient Egypt. Teller of riddles in ancient Greece. A figure often used to ward off evil in many Asian cultures, even today.

Why I'd Make a Great Mascot:

A lion's strength would intimidate other sports teams; eagle wings would help us soar to great heights; riddles would entertain fans at games and represent our academic clubs well. Warding off evil never hurts, either! In short, the sphinx has stood the test of time over millennia for many different cultures; it could do the same for our many different students, too.

"I should have known you'd go with ancient Egypt," Adam said. Jason appeared beside him.

Nadia shrugged. "I'm proud of my home country. But did you see all that other stuff I found? Isn't it cool how the sphinx has been significant in all those different cultures? And Egyptian sphinxes don't always have wings but the Greek and Asian sphinxes do, and the Greeks added the serpent's tail, which is awesome!"

Jason frowned. "I don't know if I want a sphinx on my jersey. It just seems . . . weird."

"Weird?" Nadia said. "How?"

"It's just too different," he said. "Unfamiliar."

Nadia looked him in the eye. "Hamar," she said.

He looked surprised. "Really?"

"Yup," Nadia said. After their difficulty last fall, the Nerd Patrol had come up with the code word *hamar* if Jason—or any of them—said something disrespectful. "Just because something is unfamiliar to *you* doesn't mean that it's *weird*."

"Sorry," Jason said sheepishly. "And thanks for letting me know."

Nadia reviewed all the posters again. There were some promising choices, but the sphinx was obviously the best. She dashed into the office and grabbed a ballot, marked it, and dropped it into the box.

"I bet I know which mascot you just voted for!" said a familiar voice behind her.

Nadia turned around and smiled. "I bet you do, too," she said. "I've been meaning to thank you for listening to my request about the mascot, Mr. Taylor. I know it couldn't have been easy for you."

"Not easy? Why?" asked Principal Taylor.

"You know," said Nadia. "Because you were the petunia when you were a student here."

"Oh, right," Principal Taylor said. "But we can't live in the past! Gotta move on sometime, yes?"

"Yes!" Nadia said, once again grateful that she'd spoken up about the mascot.

"You know," Principal Taylor continued. "We would have had an even dozen, but can you believe that someone nominated the poop emoji?" He shook his head. "I'm really going to have to give that Ivana Tinkle a piece of my mind!"

Twenty-four hours and four minutes later (not that Nadia was counting), Ms. Arena said the worst thing ever: The first issue of *Newsflash* would not be handed out in homeroom.

"Are you sure?" Nadia asked.

"Ms. Tovey told me there were issues at the printer," Ms. Arena said.

Ms. Tovey confirmed that in language arts. "The papers should be delivered before lunchtime, though," she said. "Actually, if a few of you could show up here right before lunch, you can pick up papers and hand them out as the students head into the cafeteria. Any volunteers?"

Nadia's hand was the first to shoot up.

Ms. Tovey counted the volunteers. "Wonderful," she said. "Now I just want to tell you how proud I am of each and every one of you. From the writers and photographers to the designers and copy editors." She smiled at Oona and Mateo. "To the crossword puzzle editors and the cartoonists. This was a group effort and you all did a fantastic job. You should congratulate yourselves."

That led the class into the inevitable shaking of one's own hand. As they did so, Nadia began to daydream about seeing her byline. She was probably going to frame the article and keep it in her room. Unless her mother wanted to hang it in the living room. She smiled and pushed up the sleeves of the red-and-orange striped sweater that Adam's mom had given her for Christmas. Was it hot in here or was all the excitement making her sweat?

There was a knock at the door and Ms. Tovey opened it. There stood Principal Taylor and Mr. Flores, the new janitor.

They stepped inside and Principal Taylor bobbed his head at the class. "Good morning, students, Ms. Tovey. I apologize for the interruption, but our new janitor, Mr. Flores, and I are going from class to class today to address an issue affecting our school. It seems very important to him, so I wanted to address it right away. Students, I'm afraid I have to give you a bit of a scolding."

"Oh no!" Mateo whispered, in mock horror. "A scolding!"

"Mr. Flores has alerted me that the littering situation here in the hallowed halls of Bridget Mason Middle has gotten out of control," Principal Taylor continued. "We're talking candy wrappers, apple cores, empty milk containers . . ."

Nadia raised an eyebrow. Was Mr. Taylor going to mention every type of garbage the students created?

". . . pizza crusts, banana peels, um, peach pits . . ." His voice trailed off. "Yogurt containers, half-eaten cookies . . ." Finally, he seemed to exhaust his list of litter.

"So. Mr. Flores and I came up with a solution that I think will be amenable to everyone. We have a pledge for you to recite. A pledge that you will put your trash where it belongs. In the trash can!" He gave a little laugh. "Will you all please stand?"

Adam turned around and mouthed "Really?" to Nadia. Even Ms. Tovey seemed to be trying not to laugh.

"I'm serious," Principal Taylor said. "Up, up, everyone."

There was the great groaning sound as a classroomful of chairs simultaneously scraped the floor.

"Now, place your hands on your hearts and repeat after me," Principal Taylor said.

Nadia sighed and slipped her hand over her heart, just under her hippo amulet.

"Okay," Principal Taylor continued. "I pledge to do my duty and put my trash where it belongs—in the garbage can."

There was some giggling, but the students all obediently repeated: "I pledge to do my duty and put my trash where it belongs—in the garbage can."

"Why don't you say the rest, Mr. Flores," said Principal Taylor. He handed the janitor a laminated piece of paper.

"Uh, um, thank you, Mr. Taylor," Mr. Flores said, looking embarrassed and a little shy. "I . . . I pledge to do my duty and never slam-dunk my rubbish from across the room, but instead place it carefully inside the trash barrel," he read. Nadia detected a Hispanic accent. She wondered if the janitor was an immigrant like she was.

Nadia suddenly realized that her new sweater wasn't just hot—it was itchy, too. She inched a finger up to scratch her collarbone. "I pledge to do my duty and . . ." she repeated. The tingly itching faded. *Ahhhh.*

"And I pledge to do my duty and pick up any refuse I may find on the floor as I go about my day. This I solemnly pledge," Mr. Flores finished.

Everyone repeated the final line. It seemed a bit redundant to Nadia, but Mr. Flores did seem to put up with a lot. All the students sat down.

"Well, um, thank you, Principal Taylor, Mr. Flores," Ms. Tovey said.

Principal Taylor took the laminated page from Mr. Flores and held it up. "This pledge will hang in the hallways by every garbage can for your reference. Read it. Learn it. Live it."

Mr. Flores nodded his head and the two left the classroom.

They spent the rest of class brainstorming for the next issue of *Newsflash*. When the end-of-class bell rang, Ms. Tovey stood by the door. "Don't forget to meet me here right before lunch to pick up your copies of the paper. And that's the scoop!"

Chapter Seven

When the bell for lunch rang, Nadia rushed to room 605. She put her stack of newspapers down on a desk and grabbed the top copy. This was it. She flipped the paper open and searched for her column. A shiver of excitement ran down her spine when she saw her name in print.

As a Matter of Fact
by Nadia Youssef

By the time you read this column, the students of Bridget Mason Middle School will have been presented with nominations for a new school mascot. Fellow students—do you know what a privilege this is? Our choices today will affect not only current students, but students for generations to come.

A mascot conveys the identity of a school and

its students without having to say a word. It needs to represent all of us. Not only our sports teams but also our astronomy club, our Irish dancing squad, and our stamp-collecting crew, to name but a few. We need a mascot that can do cartwheels on the basketball court and also offer silent support during a Model UN event. One that can celebrate with the chess club and cheer on the gymnastics team.

So before you fill out a ballot, I encourage you to ask yourself these questions: Who am I? Which mascot best represents me? But then ask these questions, too: Who are my classmates? Which mascot best represents them?

You need to make sure you're voting not for *your* school, but *our* school.

And that is a matter of fact.

Nice job, Nadia, she said to herself. Informative. To the point. She gave herself a mental pat on the back, then looked up. The room was empty—the rest of the students had already left to hand out their papers. Hurriedly, she stuck the paper into her backpack, grabbed her stack, and headed to the cafeteria. She positioned herself by the northeast entrance.

"Extra! Extra! Read all about it!" Nadia called out as kids passed by. She might as well get into the whole newsboy role.

Some kids were excited to get the paper. "Oh, cool. Thanks, Nadia," said a boy from her science class. Someone else grabbed a paper and hit his friend over the head with it. Still another took a copy and tossed it toward the trash, but missed. Mr. Flores wasn't going to like that.

When she'd handed out all her papers, she headed to

her lunch table, glancing around to see who was reading the paper. Surely someone must have read her column by now and was looking to give her a thumbs-up. But as she scanned the room, she could see Abby doing the crossword puzzle while a couple of kids devoured Adam's article, "An Interview with Bridget Mason's New Favorite Teacher, Mr. Ferrari."

Nadia had been a bit miffed when she found out Adam had decided to profile Titi, who had been her friend first, after all. She noticed a couple of kids take out their phones, probably to watch his accompanying video, "Seven Quick Questions with Mr. Ferrari."

A couple of other kids were laughing at Mateo's cartoon, which, in her opinion, wasn't all that funny. It didn't look like anybody had even gotten to the page with her column yet.

At least she'd get some love from the Nerd Patrol. She sat down at the table and looked at her friends expectantly.

"So?" she said.

"I'm totally jealous that I don't have Mr. Ferrari for social studies," said Vikram with a sigh. "He sounds awesome. Great story, Adam."

"Thanks," said Adam. "Ms. Tovey didn't seem thrilled with it." He shrugged. "But everyone else seems to love it."

Nadia stared at Vikram until he realized what she was after. "Oh yeah, I liked your article, too," he said unconvincingly.

"Yeah," said Chloe with a smile that Nadia recognized as fake. "It was great."

Nadia reached into her lunch bag and pulled out an apple. This wasn't the reception she'd been hoping for. She decided to try again.

"Exactly what did you like about my column?" she asked Chloe. She felt slightly bad, putting her friend on the spot, but shook it off.

"Oh, um," Chole said. "It was . . . interesting?"

"Interesting how?" Nadia said. Surely Chloe could find a better word than interesting. Chloe glanced around the table at the rest of the Nerd Patrol, looking for support.

"You want the truth, Nadia?" Sarah asked. "Your column was a little boring. You're so fun . . . and your article wasn't. It felt a little . . . preachy."

"Yeah," Jason said. "You could have made it more fun by adding something like a video, like Adam did with his interview with Mr. Ferrari."

"Hey, speaking of Mr. Ferrari," Vikram said, "did you hear that—"

But Nadia had heard enough about Adam's amazing interview. She stood up, mumbled a hasty goodbye to the Nerd Patrol, and headed to social studies, which she had right after lunch that day. She'd go early to see what Titi thought of her article. He'd have something positive to say.

Her footsteps echoed in the empty hallway. Titi's classroom door was open, so she poked her head inside, hoping to find him meditating. She was disappointed to discover the room was empty. But there was a sign on his desk. She stepped inside to get a better look. PRIVATE SIGN: DO NOT READ.

Nadia chuckled, then sat down at her own desk and took out her notebook and favorite pen. She pulled the newspaper out of her backpack and turned to her article to read it once more. She could sort of see what Sarah was saying about it being preachy, but everything in it was true. Students should consider all those things before voting on a mascot. She herself hadn't thought about them at first, so many kids probably hadn't, either.

She folded the newspaper and stuck it in her notebook. Soon, students started to trickle into the classroom.

"I hope we don't get Mrs. Booker as our substitute," Anna said. Mrs. Booker was the super-ancient school librarian who sometimes did last-minute subbing. "She makes everyone speak in their 'quiet voice.'"

"Substitute?" said Nadia. "What happened to Ti—I mean, Mr. Ferrari?"

"Oh, didn't you hear?" said Andrew. "In the middle of second period there was this crazy-weird sound and then he disappeared."

"Yeah—Aiden said it was the coolest magic trick he'd ever seen," said Ella. "And no one has seen him since."

Nadia frowned. Leaving his students in the middle of a class? That didn't sound like Titi at all.

"Hello, class," said a voice.

Nadia looked up. It was Coach Zuckerman, her least favorite gym teacher. He made everything into a competition, including which student had the stinkiest sneakers in gym class. Improbably enough, that student was the winner of the contest, not the loser.

"Settle down, settle down. This is my free period, so I'm not putting up with anyone's malarkey today." He shook his head. "Figures Ferrari just decides to skip out. Most popular teacher," he grumbled.

Nadia rolled her eyes. Even Coach Zuckerman had read Adam's story!

But as the coach asked them to take out their textbooks, Nadia's thoughts turned back to Titi. She grabbed her amulet like she always did when she was worried.

"I hope he doesn't need my help," she whispered to herself.

"Today we will learn about the fascinating world of . . ." Coach Zuckerman looked down at Mr. Ferrari's planner. "Roman aqueducts?" he said. "Hoo boy." He sighed and began to read aloud: "Aqueducts were used to transport water from one place to another—" He paused. A couple of kids had started whispering. "Listen up, everyone. There will be a quiz on this."

A quiz! Nadia opened her notebook, the newspaper still tucked inside it. As she clicked her pen, she thought she saw something move. She looked down, and to her utter amazement, a tiny animated version of Titi was on the newspaper, peeking up over the top of her notebook! He was waving at Nadia and jumping up and down, just like he used to when she'd first freed him from the amulet last fall.

"NADIA!" Titi shouted.

Nadia slapped her hand down on top of Titi to silence him. A couple of students whipped their heads around to stare.

"Fly," Nadia said. "Got it."

She slowly lifted her hand back up, then stared down at the page. She slid the newspaper out of her notebook and put her finger to her lips, hoping Titi would understand her message: *I'm in class, dude. You can't be talking.* Then she widened her eyes to add: *What the heck is going on?*

Titi apparently got the message, because he started pushing letters from her article together to form a message.

60

I somehow got sent back to the amulet! and now I'm out but stuck on paper again. Help!

"Nadia Youssef, please put the newspaper away," barked the gym teacher. Nadia shoved it back in her notebook and slammed it shut.

"Um . . . I need to be excused," she said.

Coach Zuckerman didn't look pleased, but he nodded. Nadia scooped up her notebook and stepped out of the classroom.

She could see Mr. Flores at the far end of the hallway, heading in her direction. Not knowing where else to go, she ducked into the girls' bathroom and locked herself in a stall. Then she crouched down to look on either side to make sure she was alone.

That done, she flipped open the notebook to the newspaper. But Titi was nowhere to be found. That's when she remembered that closing the notebook used to send him back to the amulet. She grabbed the hippo and said "help," just like old times.

Titi appeared on the paper again, right next to her article.

"Hey," Nadia said. "Did you read my article? What did you think?"

"Right," Titi said, annoyance on his face. "Because I had so much time to *read* while wondering why I'm STUCK ON PAPER AGAIN!"

"Sorry," Nadia said. "What happened? Did I somehow send you back to the amulet? I didn't know that was possible."

"It must be part of the original spell," said Titi. "Since

you can release me from the amulet, I guess it makes sense that you can put me back, too."

Nadia thought for a moment. "But how did it happen? What could I possibly have done to trap you in the amulet again?"

Titi shook his head. "Beats me."

Nadia thought for another moment, then gasped.

"I know how I got you out again!" she said. "I was holding the amulet and wondered out loud if you needed my help." She bit her lip. "But we really should figure out how I sent you there in the first place. I want to make sure that never happens again."

"You bet your sweet sarcophagus we're going to figure that out," Titi said. He leaned up against the side of her column. "But it was weird when I was in there this time. Different. I'm pretty sure I was in the front part of the hippo. And there was this strange smell. Kind of spicy. It was familiar, but I couldn't put my finger on it."

"Well, at least it didn't smell like hippo hiney," joked Nadia.

"Har-dee-har-har," said Titi. "Three thousand years in a hippo butt is nothing to joke about, Nadia."

But Nadia couldn't help herself. "Sorry for being so cheeky."

Titi rolled his eyes. "Just get me off this paper, will you? I've got to get back to class before Zuckerman bores everyone to death."

"We may have already lost a few," said Nadia. "So you

think you just need to help me solve seven problems again to become human?"

"Can't hurt to try," Titi said. "Got any math problems? That would be quick."

Luckily Nadia's phone was in her back pocket. She quickly looked up some difficult problems, wrote them down one by one, and had Titi help her solve them.

As he was finishing up the last one, Nadia opened the stall door. She placed the newspaper down on one of the sinks. In a moment, POOF! Titi reappeared in his human form. She stifled a laugh. He was sitting in the sink, his legs dangling over the side.

He looked around, bewilderedly. "Great Giza, am I in the ladies' room, Nadia?"

"Sorry," she said with a shrug. "I didn't know where else to go."

He boosted himself out of the sink and stood up. Nadia didn't have the nerve to tell him that his butt was wet.

After sticking his head out the doorway and looking both ways, Titi sprinted out of the bathroom.

Nadia was in no rush to see how annoyed Coach Zuckerman was going to be by Titi's sudden reappearance. She grabbed her notebook and walked down the hallway back to the classroom as slowly as she could.

The magician kicked a chair over. Plan Number Three had worked . . . until it didn't. He hadn't known how to get the girl to send the teacher back to the amulet. But then he'd heard her redheaded friend talking backward one day and it clicked: In ancient Egypt, they used backward spells all the time. Perhaps he needed the girl to say the magic word backward to reverse the hippo spell. It had been tricky, but he'd figured out how to get her to say it.

It had been even trickier to get her to say the teacher's secret name in close proximity to the backward magic word. That made sure that it was the teacher who got sent back and not him. But he'd figured out how to do that, too. Luckily, the teacher had confessed his secret name to Khefren when they were young and foolish and best friends. The only thing he hadn't been able to pull off was sending the teacher directly to the hippo's hindquarters, as he had done the first time around.

Not that it mattered. The girl had freed the teacher so quickly, he hadn't had time to get the amulet from her so he could destroy it while the teacher was inside.

The magician decided he'd have to move on to Plan Number Four. This one might take some time . . . but he loved a good challenge.

The mascot contest was an interesting development, and the girl seemed extra excited about the newspaper. He rubbed his hands together with anticipation. He had the playing pieces and the game; now he just needed the perfect strategy.

He ripped open a bag of honey roasted peanuts and shook some into his mouth. He was down to only two bags of nuts a day. Things were looking up.

Chapter Eight

Nadia must have walked past the bulletin board by the main office thirty-four times on Tuesday, trying to get a sense of which mascots students were voting for. One time she heard a couple of football players talking about the rhinoceros, and an artsy kid swear he'd never vote for anything so "aggro." Then the football players had accused the artsy kid of making fun of them, and, well, Nadia wasn't sure what happened because she booked it out of there. She hoped there weren't similar conversations happening about the sphinx.

On Wednesday afternoon, Nadia plopped down in her seat in math class, her last class that day. In half an hour, she'd know whether the sphinx was a finalist.

She watched as her classmates Angelo and Mike walked into the classroom, chatting. Nadia flipped open her notebook, started doodling, and listened.

"So did you vote?" Angelo asked.

"Nah, I ran out of time. I've been busy with basketball practice and everything," said Mike. "It's just the first round of voting, though, right? I'll vote in the final election."

"Don't tell your boy Jason you didn't vote for his mascot!" said Angelo, punching Mike in the arm. "I'm kinda hoping that pizza is a finalist. That would be awesome. But yeah, I didn't vote, either."

Nadia rolled her eyes. How hard was it to check a box on a piece of paper?

"Hey," Angelo said to Mike. "You joining Mr. Ferrari's magic club?"

Nadia's ears perked up. Since when did Titi have a magic club? She had asked if he wanted to do a comic book dive to help her with a science assignment the day before and he said he didn't have time. Was that why? Nadia felt a little prick of jealousy.

Class began, but she had trouble concentrating—because of the magic club, yes, but mostly in anticipation of the mascot results. With five minutes left to go in class, the loudspeaker switched on with a hiss.

Yadda, yadda, yadda . . . Finally, Taylor got to the good stuff.

"The two mascot finalists are . . ." Principal Taylor's voice took on the timbre of a WWE announcer: "THE HAWK AND . . . THE SPHINX!"

Nadia let out a little yelp. She'd done it! A couple of students turned around and smiled.

"Congratulations to Nadia Youssef and Mia Catacutan, who nominated the sphinx and the hawk," Principal Taylor continued. "But students, this is everyone's contest now. These next two weeks are your chance to show your fellow students which mascot you think best represents our school. Claim the sphinx or hawk as if it's already your mascot and show your school spirit with posters on the walls, raps in the hallways, sonnets on the bulletin boards—don't be afraid to get creative!" He explained that the final vote would be in two weeks. "But I must say, students, voter turnout for this primary was rather . . . weak. Let's work on that for the final vote." His voice got louder, as if he was super close to the mic. "Now, let's show that school SPIIIIRRIIIIIIIIIIIIIT!!"

Nadia beamed. And—she couldn't help it—she did a little happy dance in her chair.

The next day Nadia met up with the Nerd Patrol after school. Everyone had already congratulated her about the sphinx. Even Adam, Chloe, and Jason, whose nominations were beat out. (In Adam's words, "The school wasn't ready for the awesomeness of pizza. They weren't ready to be pizza.")

"So what's the plan, Nadia?" Sarah asked. "To show your school spiiirriiiiiiiiit for the sphinx?"

"I have some ideas I'm working on," Nadia said. "But you should all feel free to show your support for the sphinx, too, like Taylor said."

"I've got something cooking," Vikram said.

"Cool," Nadia said. Then she asked Adam if she could borrow the comic book and headed to Titi's classroom. She wanted his help with a sphinx idea.

"Heavens to Mentuhotep!" Titi cheered when he saw her. "You did it!"

Nadia grinned. "I know! But now I need to start campaigning. I want to make some 'Fun Sphinx Facts' posters to hang around the school and was thinking we could do a comic book dive to gather some. You free right now?"

Titi shook his head. "Principal Taylor had a request from some students to start a magic club with me as the adviser, and the first meeting is today. It starts in"—he glanced up at the classroom clock—"five minutes."

Nadia's face fell. So it was true. She knew Titi was already busy with lesson planning. When would he ever have time for comic book dives?

Someone knocked on the door.

"Hey, Mr. Ferrari!" said an eighth grader as he burst into the classroom. He reached into the back pocket of his jeans and pulled out . . . Nadia blinked . . . a large bouquet of flowers. "Ta-da!"

"Cleopatra's needles!" Titi cried. "Nice job, Nicolas!"

Kids began pouring into the room carrying capes, top hats, and magic wands, everyone chattering excitedly.

Nadia turned to Titi, puzzled. "But you do *real* magic," she whispered. "How are you supposed to teach magic tricks?"

Titi pointed to the stack of library books sitting on his

desk. They all had the word magic on the spine. One read: *Magic 101: Learning the Basics to Mystify and Delight Your Friends and Family.*

"Research!" Titi said. He grabbed one of the books off his desk. "Actually, Nadia, Mrs. Booker said she needed this one back. Would you mind returning it to the library for me?"

That prick of jealousy appeared again, sharper this time. Now she was Titi's assistant?

"Um, okay," Nadia said, taking the book. "Would you maybe want to get together this weekend to work on the mascot stuff?"

"Oooh, I can't," Titi said. "Magician-Con is this weekend and I have tickets for all three days. Conjurer level, all-access no less! Can you believe they have a Super Seminar on ancient Egyptian magic? I'm as excited as an ibis at an all-you-can-eat crustacean buffet! Can I get a rain check?"

That prick of jealousy grew into a spiky ball.

"Yeah, sure," Nadia said, trying to keep her voice neutral. She held up the book. "I'll make sure Mrs. Booker gets this." Then she turned and left the classroom before Titi could say anything else disappointing.

She made her way down the hallway, the spiky ball growing bigger. Soon it was joined by a lump in her throat.

"Get it together, Nadia," she muttered to herself as she approached the library and dropped the book in the return slot. "Titi's got a life. So what?"

But she was suddenly overcome with how much she had to do. The sphinx stuff. Her second newspaper article, which she hadn't even started. Plus a math test next week. She'd been counting on Titi to help her study for that, too.

Titi had said he'd be there for her that first day of school. Those were his exact words.

"Everything okay, Nadia?" a voice said.

Nadia looked up, realizing she was still holding the return slot open, lost in thought. She quickly let go.

"Oh, um, I—"

Principal Taylor gestured inside the library to a nearby table and chairs. "Would you like to talk?"

Um, not really, Nadia thought. *But can I say no to the principal?* She walked inside and tentatively took a seat. Principal Taylor sat down and made a steeple of his fingers, holding them close to his face.

"I know you've got a lot on your plate right now, Nadia. How are you handling it all?"

Nadia wasn't sure how to answer that. *I've been abandoned by my magical friend who happens to be one of your teachers* probably wouldn't fly.

"Is there anything I can do to help?" Principal Taylor continued. "I was in middle school once, you know. I've had my own share of preadolescent woes."

Nadia grimaced. Who said stuff like *preadolescent woes?* But Principal Taylor did seem to want to help. And she knew (from looking in his yearbook) that he was even nerdier in middle school than she was. He probably *did* know what it felt like to have drama with friends and schoolwork. And,

she realized, unlike Titi, he had time to listen to her. Nadia
took a breath. Where to start?

"It's friend stuff . . ."

Principal Taylor nodded. Nadia continued.

"This one friend used to help me out all the time. I
helped them, too. We were a team, you know?"

Principal Taylor nodded again.

"But now . . ." Nadia bit her lip. "I don't know. They've
gotten kind of flaky—"

Principal Taylor sighed so loudly Nadia stopped talking.

He smiled at her, opened his mouth to say something, and then closed it again. Then he seemed to force a smile onto his face. Nadia fidgeted in her seat. This was awkward with a capital *A*.

"I'll tell you something I've learned, Nadia," Principal Taylor said. "It's not going to be easy to hear."

"Okay . . ." Nadia said.

"Most people don't help other people just for the sake of being nice. That's not how the world works. Now, this friend—when they helped you before, did they get anything out of it? You said you helped them, too?"

Nadia frowned. Of course Titi had gotten something out of helping her last fall—his freedom. Nadia had always thought that Titi would have helped her out anyway, though; that's just who Titi was. But she answered Taylor's question honestly.

"Yeah, they got something out of it," Nadia said. "A pretty big something."

Principal Taylor had a look of pity on his face that she didn't like, not one bit. "Nadia, it sounds to me like this 'friend' was only a friend until they had no more use for you. It sounds like they may have used you."

Nadia shook her head. "No, that's not right. This friend said they were happy to help—"

"I'm afraid many people lie, too, Nadia. In fact, I'd say most people do."

Nadia frowned again. She didn't lie. The Nerd Patrol didn't lie. But Principal Taylor clearly had more life experience. Maybe adults were different? Then again, her parents were adults and they didn't lie to her, at least not that she knew of. She'd known them her whole life, though. She'd known Titi only a few months.

"Well," Principal Taylor said, standing up and snapping Nadia out of her thoughts. "I hope this little heart-to-heart was helpful."

"Oh, yeah, of course," Nadia said. She stood, too, suddenly realizing that not every principal would take the time to talk with a student like this. "Thanks. You're a good principal, Mr. Taylor."

"Thank you, Nadia," he said. "I'm always here for my students."

Chapter Nine

Poster."

Sarah handed Nadia a poster.

"Tape."

Sarah handed Nadia some tape.

Nadia stretched her arm up to stick the poster above the lockers. When she couldn't reach, she tried jumping, but couldn't get it to stick.

"Maybe Mr. Flores has a stepladder," Sarah suggested. She nodded toward the janitor, who was rummaging around in a storage closet down the hall. Nadia ran over.

"Um, hi, Mr. Flores. I'm Nadia. It's nice to officially meet you." She stuck out her hand for a handshake.

Mr. Flores gave her a funny look but shook her hand, then went back to rummaging around.

"Do you think I could borrow a stepladder or . . ."

Nadia peered over his shoulder into the closet. There were a bunch of buckets on the floor. "Or a bucket, maybe? I want to hang some flyers and seem to be vertically challenged."

Mr. Flores again didn't say anything, but motioned that she should help herself to a bucket.

"Thanks!" Nadia said, grabbing one.

She ran back to Sarah.

"Mr. Flores doesn't say much, does he?" Nadia said. She stepped onto the overturned bucket and stuck the poster up. She'd had to resort to an internet search for her fun facts. She was sure a comic book dive would have given her even better ones, but she was proud of what she'd come up with.

"He sure had a lot to say with that no-littering pledge," Sarah said.

Nadia laughed, glancing at one of the pledges posted over a nearby garbage can. She'd almost forgotten about that.

The friends hung the rest of the posters around school. They put them in the cafeteria, the art room, the music room, above drinking fountains, even in the bathroom stalls. Every student at Bridget Mason was going to know how awesome the sphinx was. Nadia was delighted, too, that there was a giant banner in the art room with a gorgeously painted sphinx on it. Clearly, someone else was already inspired by her mascot.

"Hey, Sarah," said Nadia as they hung the last poster. "Did you see that hawk banner?"

"Huh?" said Sarah. "What banner?"

"Exactly," Nadia said, smiling. "Here we are two days

Fun Sphinx Fact: The eyes of the Great Sphinx of Giza in Egypt are six feet tall!

after the finalists were announced—and there's nothing from the hawk supporters. I'm thinking the sphinx is a shoo-in."

"Well, don't print the T-shirts yet," Sarah said as they walked out the front doors of the school. "There's still a week and a half until the vote."

"Fair enough," Nadia said. She waved to Baba, who was waiting in the car, then turned back to Sarah. "Thanks for helping me. I'll see you tomorrow." The Nerds were going ice-skating at the seasonal outdoor ice rink at the Santa Monica Pier. It would be Nadia's first time ice-skating ever!

Sarah nodded. "See you!"

The sounds of carnival rides and ocean waves washed over Nadia. The sun shone brightly overhead. But Nadia was cold. Which made sense—she was lying flat on her back on the ice.

"Ahhhhhhhh," she groaned.

Skates flashed by as people swerved around her. *Ice skates are actually torture devices*, Nadia decided. *Two giant razor blades strapped to an uncomfortable pair of prairie girl boots.*

Vikram looked down at her sadly. "You were doing great until those Weasels knocked into you."

"Vikram, that's mean," said Nadia, sitting up. "I don't think they did it on purpose."

Vikram laughed. "No, they actually *are* weasels—the Westside Weasels. See that kid's sweatshirt? That's their mascot."

Chloe extended a hand to help Nadia up.

The Westside Weasels vs. the Bridget Mason Sphinxes, Nadia thought. Or was the plural of "sphinx" also "sphinx"? She'd have to look that up. Either way, it sounded way better than Westside Weasels vs. the Bridget Mason Petunias.

Adam and Sarah skated up to them. "You yako?" Adam asked.

"Yeah," Nadia said. "I'm okay. The only thing that got hurt is my dignity. Again." This was the third time she'd fallen. "Can we get some hot chocolate or something?"

They headed to the snack bar. Once everyone ordered, Vikram told them he'd been working on a papier-mâché sphinx head.

"Amazing!" Nadia said. "When do you plan to debut that?"

"Not sure yet," Vikram said. "I was thinking maybe . . ."

He kept talking, but Nadia didn't hear what he said. She was too busy squinting across the ice rink. There was somebody waving at her.

It was Titi!

He was supposed to be at Magician-Con. She found herself feeling a bit annoyed. Now he had time for her? When she was finally out having fun with her friends? And she didn't even need his help anymore, she realized. Vikram and that art student and probably countless others were already doing awesome things to promote the sphinx.

But Titi wasn't smiling, and his waving was more frantic than enthusiastic.

"Uh, it's great to hear about the sphinx stuff," Nadia said to her friends. "In fact, I'm so inspired that I think I'll go home right now and make more posters. Adam, I forgot my pencil case in my locker. Maybe I can borrow some pencils from your house?"

"You don't have any pencils at home?" Adam said, but Nadia tipped her head in Titi's direction.

"Ohhh," Adam said. "Yeah, totally, we can stop by my house for pencils. Later, nerds!"

They quickly returned their rented skates and jogged over to Titi.

He didn't even say hello. "Adam, please tell me you have the comic book!"

Adam nodded. "Always!" He pulled it out of his pocket.

"What's wrong?" Nadia asked Titi.

Titi took a deep breath. "Something is rotten in the Valley of the Kings. I've been trying to piece things together ever since I got sent back to the amulet. Then something at Magician-Con gave me an idea. I have to get to the bottom of this—now."

"What do you mean—" Nadia started to say.

But Titi was racing away from the ice rink toward the end of the pier overlooking the water. He motioned for them to follow him. When they reached a secluded spot, Titi held up the comic book. "Hold on to your hats!"

WHOOSH!

Nadia sat down heavily on a bench near the railing of the pier.

Adam stared ahead, slowly shaking his head. "So . . . what . . . does that . . . ?" He could barely force the words out.

Titi sat on the bench next to Nadia, his head in his hands.

"Let me see if I have this right," Nadia said. "Your BFF turned bully—Khefren is his name?—was also imprisoned in the amulet those three thousand years, but you had no idea."

Titi slowly raised his head. "Remember how I said earlier, Nadia, that the front half of the hippo smelled funny? And that I recognized the scent but I couldn't put my finger on it? I had been wondering—if I was stuck in the tail end those three millennia, was someone else stuck in the head? Then someone at Magician-Con mentioned myrrh as an ancient tool of magic, and, well, our little trip down memory lane just confirmed it: I did have company, and it was Khefren."

"And then you had to do all the hard work on the seven solutions before both of you got the satisfaction of becoming fully human." Nadia gave a little harrumph of annoyance. That sounded like every group project she'd ever worked on.

Titi stood and stared out at the ocean.

"So where is he?" asked Adam. "If he's not in the amulet anymore, does that mean—"

"He would be hard to miss if he were among us," Titi said. "You saw him in the comic—he's absurdly tall and

85

very thin with that dark wig—" Titi stopped. He'd turned very pale.

"What is it, Titi?" Nadia asked.

"The chandelier," Titi said. "In Memphis. I bet that was him."

"I thought the police said it was an accident," Adam said.

"Yeah," Titi said. "I heard some scary stories about Khefren causing 'accidents' when someone displeased him. Someone told me that the royal chef once made some food that didn't agree with him. Poof! No one ever saw the poor chef again."

"But you're both free," Nadia said. "Why would Khefren care what happens to you now?"

"For the love of Isis, Nadia," Titi said. "If someone caused you to be imprisoned for three thousand years, wouldn't you want a little something called revenge?"

"What?!" Adam said. "Titi, you're not the reason Khefren was imprisoned! What happened was all his fault. You can't blame yourself!"

"No, of course not," Titi said. "But the fact is, he wouldn't have been imprisoned if I hadn't shown up that day in front of the palace."

"Titi's right," Nadia said.

Adam started pacing. "Titi, you didn't even get a scratch when that chandelier fell on you. Khefren can't hurt you; you're immortal. So if he wants revenge, how would he—"

Nadia gasped and turned to Titi. "If Khefren can't kill

86

you in real life, the next best thing would be . . ." She pointed to her necklace.

"Trapping me in the amulet again," Titi said. "And if Khefren—"

"Got his hands on the amulet while you were inside," Nadia continued, "he could somehow destroy it and—"

"TITI WOULD BE GONE FOREVER!" Adam shouted.

"Sweet baby Anubis!" Titi cried.

"Well, there's only one thing to do," Nadia said. She stood up and took off the amulet. She would miss it, but this was Titi's life they were talking about. "Goodbye, dear hippo," she said softly. And before she could think twice, she tossed it off the pier into the ocean.

Titi's eyes went wide. "Did you just . . . Oh, blustering beetles!" And before their unbelieving eyes, he cannonballed off the pier into the water below.

Chapter Ten

What the—" Nadia and Adam exchanged alarmed looks, then dashed down the stairs to the beach.

Nadia shaded her eyes with her hand and scanned the water. "Where is he?" she asked worriedly. "Oh, this is all my fault. He's been under for way too long. Should we find a lifeguard?"

"I see him!" Adam shouted.

"What is he doing?" Nadia asked.

"Looks like . . . the backstroke," Adam said with a strangled laugh.

After Titi emerged from the water, holding the amulet aloft in victory, Nadia gave him a big hug, getting soaked in the process. "I was so worried!" she cried. "You were underwater for so long!"

"Did you forget that I'm immortal? I could stay

underwater all day if I wanted to. It was wild down there, though. I had to fight off an angry octopus who wanted to keep the amulet for itself."

"Really?" said Adam.

"Nah," answered Titi. "But I *did* step on a flounder."

Nadia laughed, glad to see Titi joking around a bit.

"You're okay, though, right?" Adam asked.

"I am," said Titi. "But you know what would make me feel better?"

"What?" asked Adam.

"Cotton candy," he answered. "The blue kind."

"Don't they all taste the same?" Adam said. He caught a look from Nadia. "Okay. One blue cotton candy, coming right up!" He took off for the pier.

Titi sat on a log, took off his shoes, and began wringing out his socks.

"So why exactly did you dive after the amulet?" Nadia asked. "If it was gone in the ocean forever, Khefren wouldn't be able to trap you in it. Problem solved."

Titi shook his head. "We have to look at the bigger picture, Nadia. Getting rid of the amulet keeps me safe, but Khefren . . . he'll just get angrier. If he can't hurt me, he's going to look for other people to harm. That's just how he is."

Nadia nodded. That made sense, and was really scary. She sat down next to Titi. "I'm sorry," she said. "I just wanted to keep you safe." Titi might not have been there for her lately, but she certainly didn't want anything bad to happen to him.

Fun Fact: Machine-spun cotton candy was invented by a dentist (with the help of a candy maker) in 1897.

Titi softened. "I know, kiddo," he said. "Look on the bright side, though—now that we know Khefren is here, we can do something about it. And that's really why I dove after the amulet. It's the only way Khefren can get rid of me, but it's also the only way *we* can get rid of Khefren. He's immortal, too, you know."

Nadia sighed. Of course.

Titi handed Nadia the hippo and she put it back around her neck. "What do we do now?" she asked.

"Oh," Titi said. "You mean how do we find and trap an evil magician who has been plotting his revenge for more than three thousand years?" He shrugged. "Shouldn't be that hard."

Monday was Martin Luther King Jr. Day and a day off from school. Nadia attended a community celebration at City Hall with her parents, then told them she was meeting up with Adam at a nearby coffee shop, which was at least partly true.

"We'll pick you up in an hour," Mama said. "Bye, habibti."

"Farting is such sweet sorrow," said Baba with an impish grin.

"Baba!" Nadia gasped, looking around to make sure no one had heard.

She walked the couple of blocks to the shop. Adam and Titi were already there, iced teas in front of them, though it didn't seem like Titi had touched his. He was back to looking incredibly anxious. When an ice cream truck barreled by outside, playing its cheerful music, Titi nearly jumped out of his skin.

Nadia sat down and opened her notebook. She and Adam spent the next hour asking Titi questions about Khefren and brainstorming about what the evil magician's strategy for revenge might be.

CONCLUSIONS:

- I (Nadia) am probably the only one who can send Titi or Khefren back to the amulet (since I'm the one who released them).

- We think Khefren's goal is to get me to send Titi back to the amulet so he can destroy it. To do that, he needs me and Titi in roughly the same place at the same time. I never sent Titi a postcard telling him about the open teaching position at Bridget Mason—Khefren must have sent it pretending he was me. Now both Titi and I are at Bridget Mason every day.

- Khefren would also want to be at Bridget Mason or close by Bridget Mason. We, therefore, think he might be posing as someone at or near the school. Probably by taking over their body—he's too tall and thin to disguise himself otherwise.

- We assume that when I sent Titi back to the amulet by accident, it was actually Khefren somehow tricking me into sending him back. But we haven't yet figured out HOW exactly he tricked me. We will keep brainstorming to figure out how he did this.

OUR PLAN:

- ADAM AND NADIA: Investigate the suspects (see next page).

- TITI: Keep an eye out for suspicious behavior; continue researching ancient magic.

- NADIA: Guard the hippo amulet with my life, because after all, Titi's life depends on it. But also: DO NOT touch it.

At least Nadia had already figured out that last part—she'd wrapped the hippo in some yarn she found in her crafting drawer. It looked ridiculous, but cute. And most importantly, it would keep her from accidentally sending Titi back.

On the next page, Nadia had written down the suspects they had identified.

- LUNCH LADY, MRS. FARLEY

Suspicious behavior: Seems overly interested in Mr. Ferrari and his whereabouts. Recently asked Adam what time Mr. F. usually arrives at school.

- GYM TEACHER, COACH ZUCKERMAN

Suspicious behavior: Sarcastic "favorite teacher" comment; seems obsessed with smells; all around general rudeness.

- LANGUAGE ARTS TEACHER, MS. TOVEY

Suspicious behavior: Possible irrational anger at Mr. Ferrari, reason undetermined.

"And that's it," Nadia said, slamming the notebook shut. Titi jumped. She stood up. "Titi, you be careful. We'll start our investigation tomorrow."

Titi nodded and turned to go. Adam and Nadia watched him walk away, his shoulders sagging.

"*Roop* guy," said Adam.

"He didn't say 'blustering beetles' even once," Nadia said with a sigh. She hoped they found Khefren soon, if only so Titi could start being Titi again.

Chapter Eleven

The next day, bright and early, Nadia and Adam walked to school in silence, the gravity of the situation weighing on them. They parted ways at the school entrance. Nadia headed to the cafeteria and Adam to the gym to find Coach Zuckerman.

"Good morning, Mrs. Farley," Nadia called out as she approached the counter. "I'll take a blueberry muffin, please."

Mrs. Farley smiled and handed her an extra-large muffin, studded with blueberries. "How is my favorite sixth grader doing?"

"I'm good," said Nadia, pulling out a big fat blueberry and popping it into her mouth. "That new social studies teacher is keeping us all very entertained."

Mrs. Farley frowned as she handed Nadia a napkin. "I don't know what to think of that guy."

Nadia plastered on a confused expression. "You don't?"

Mrs. Farley shook her head. "He said he forgot his wallet and couldn't pay for his chimichangas, so I told him I would cover it for him. Seven bucks. That was two weeks ago!" She pursed her lips. "Do you think he's avoiding me?"

Nadia almost laughed, she was so relieved that Mrs. Farley was just plain old Mrs. Farley. "I guarantee he's not. I bet he'll pay you back today."

Mrs. Farley smiled. "That's good news."

Nadia updated Adam on the lunch lady during homeroom.

"I'm pretty sure it's not Zuckerman, either," Adam said. "I asked a bunch of fake questions pretending I was considering profiling him in the paper and it turns out he's just grumpy about everything, not just Ferrari."

That left Ms. Tovey.

"Get this, though," Adam said to Nadia. "There was hawk stuff plastered all over the locker room—a big banner that said 'Future home of the Hawks! Go out there and fly!' and some posters and stuff, too. Apparently the Hawkeyes were campaigning at all the sports events this weekend, which makes sense. Mia's on the volleyball team."

"The Hawkeyes?" Nadia said.

"That's what the hawk supporters are calling themselves," Adam said.

"Sheesh," Nadia said. "Sounds like we need to up our sphinx game. But first, Tovey. Don't forget—class is in the computer lab today."

"All right, students," Ms. Tovey said during third period. "We have a special guest coming to class later, but right now, I want to know how things are coming along for next week's edition of *Newsflash*."

Students started giving updates. Andrew was writing about the upcoming book fair and Maddie was covering the new cafeteria menu.

"I'd like to write a feature on the new school clubs," Adam said, "including Mr. Ferrari's magic club." He quickly glanced at Nadia. They watched Ms. Tovey carefully for her reaction.

"That's an excellent idea!" Ms. Tovey said. She walked closer to Adam and lowered her voice. "I admit I was a little skeptical about Mr. Ferrari at first—he borrowed my pashmina scarf for one of his historical costumes and didn't return it for a week. But when he brought it back, it was freshly ironed and folded, and revealed a bouquet of flowers when I opened it up!" Ms. Tovey blushed. "Those magic tricks are very charming!"

Nadia rolled her eyes at Adam. Ms. Tovey didn't have evil plans for Titi. She had a crush on him!

"Abby, Nadia," Ms. Tovey said, walking back to the front of the classroom. "What about you two? What are you planning for our second edition?"

Nadia sat up straighter in her seat. She'd hardly thought about her article all weekend, what with the whole evil-magician-on-the-loose thing. But she'd come up with an idea this morning—she would write about yesterday's MLK celebration and add a link to volunteer opportunities for students.

"I was really inspired by the MLK event at City Hall yesterday," Abby said. "I'd like to write an article about it."

"Terrific idea," said Ms. Tovey. "Go for it." She turned to Nadia. "What was your idea, Nadia?"

Nadia sighed. "Never mind." Her palms felt sweaty all of a sudden. The mascot stuff, her column, and that math test. Plus, they'd just ruled out all their suspects and it wasn't even lunchtime.

"Well, I'm sure you'll think of something," Ms. Tovey said. "You have almost a week until the deadline. No pressure."

Nadia felt a weight lifted off her shoulders. Maybe they could catch Khefren and then she could worry about her column!

There was a knock. Ms. Tovey grinned. "Our special guest is here!" She opened the door to reveal Mrs. Booker.

"Is now a good time?" the librarian asked in her hushed voice.

"Of course, Mrs. Booker!" Ms. Tovey exclaimed; then she lowered her voice when she saw Mrs. Booker's disapproval. "Thanks so much for taking the time to come to our class today." She turned to the students. "I've asked Mrs. Booker to talk about the importance of checking your sources when researching your articles."

Nadia and Oona shared a look. This was what Ms. Tovey was so excited about?

Mrs. Booker nodded. "Thank you, Ms. Tovey. Now, many of you know that I've been the librarian here at Bridget Mason for more than twenty years. But before that, I taught journalism at a community college. And before *that*, I spent fifteen years on the education beat of the *West End Weekly* newspaper. And let me tell you, a reporter is only as good as her sources!"

"I wonder if they chiseled their stories onto stone tablets back then?" whispered Noah, who was sitting behind Nadia.

Nadia tried her hardest to keep a straight face. She knew, very well, that grown-ups did not appreciate jokes about their age. Mrs. Booker might even raise her voice if she heard that comment.

"Now, my stint as a reporter came prior to the internet," Mrs. Booker continued. "It was a lot easier to make sure your sources were credible back then. Did your information come from a book, a magazine, a newspaper, or maybe an interview transcript? Those sources were all very concrete—you could hold them in your hands. The author's name and credentials were right there, in print. The publisher's name was there, too. It was easier to know if you could trust the information to be factual.

"I don't envy you kids. You've got the whole world at your fingertips as soon as you open a web browser. Now, what do you do if you find yourself wondering about a random question? Like . . . how many almonds a person should consume in one day, for instance. What would you do to find that answer?"

"Ask Nadia?" Mateo said, sending a big smile Nadia's way. Nadia laughed along with the rest of the class. Jason had once called her "Human Google," which she had taken as a compliment, of course.

"Well, Nadia," Mrs. Booker said, "do you know how many almonds a person should eat in a day?"

"Um," Nadia said, a bit distracted by the oddly specific question. "I don't."

"Fabulous!" said Mrs. Booker. "I mean, in this case, I'm glad you don't know. Because class—what would we do to find out?"

Andrew raised his hand. "Look it up? Do an internet search?"

"Of course!" Mrs. Booker said. "The internet is an endless treasure trove of information." She shook her head as she stared off into space. "The internet is a true marvel, isn't it, Ms. Tovey?"

"Oh, um, I suppose so," Ms. Tovey said.

Nadia giggled. Ms. Tovey was younger than Mama and Baba. She probably didn't remember life without the internet, either. For a librarian, Mrs. Booker sure was clueless sometimes.

"Anyway," Mrs. Booker said. "Not all information on the internet is created equal. As reporters—and as human beings living in a civilized society, I might add—it's your responsibility to know which information you can trust and which you can't."

"Sounds like a lot of work," Mateo blurted out.

"Ah, it can feel like that," Mrs. Booker said. "But it doesn't have to. Who loves scavenger hunts?"

A bunch of hands shot up, including Nadia's. A few kids also shouted out, "I do!"

"Shhhhhhhh," Mrs. Booker said. "Quiet voices, please."

She held up a stack of papers. "We're going to go on an internet scavenger hunt. I have worksheets for you. For each site you visit, you'll give or take away points based on whether the site is trustworthy or not. I have all those reasons listed out here. You have twenty minutes to find two sites with six or more points—trustworthy sites. And two sites with three or less points—untrustworthy sites. Ms. Tovey is passing out the worksheets. Here's your subject: Is the Dewey decimal system obsolete?"

There were a couple of groans.

Mrs. Booker held up her hand. "I know," she said. "It's a very controversial topic. But timely, too. Ready, set, start researching!"

Nadia had already opened up the web browser by the time Ms. Tovey handed her the worksheet. She skimmed the assignment. They were supposed to add a point for things like a website having been updated recently; for it being an organization they knew to be credible outside the internet; for all external links also being credible; for the main purpose of the site to be to share facts, not opinions; for there to be a physical mailing address listed on the site; and a few other things.

They were supposed to subtract a point if a website

was biased toward a specific point of view; contained many spelling errors or broken links or no external links at all; or its main purpose was to sell something.

It took longer than Nadia expected to find two trustworthy sites and two untrustworthy ones. *Whew!* It turned out that checking for all those things was time-consuming, and, surprisingly, it was easy to get distracted and fall down a Dewey decimal rabbit hole.

"Well, thank you, Mrs. Booker, for sharing your wisdom and experience with us," Ms. Tovey said.

The bell rang and everyone packed up their things to go. Adam and Nadia walked out together.

"Oh, Nadia," Mrs. Booker called. "I've been meaning to ask you. Is that an ancient Egyptian amulet you're wearing?" She lifted her glasses and peered at the hippo. "My goodness," she said, looking Nadia in the eye. "That is quite a special piece of antiquity for such a young girl to be wearing, isn't it?"

Nadia took a step back.

"I have a keen interest in ancient Egypt, you know," Mrs. Booker said. "Ever since I wrote a piece on the touring King Tut exhibit back in '78."

"That's . . . cool," Nadia said, not knowing what else to say.

Adam sidled up to her after the librarian left. "So which one of us is going to spy on her?"

"I was thinking you," Nadia said, not missing a beat. "Just in case she tries to get her hands on the amulet. She seems a little too interested in it, you know?"

"Sey," Adam said. "I'll guess I'll study in the library after school."

"Hey, I'm glad you're all here," Nadia said as she approached her locker before lunch. The Nerd Patrol, plus a handful of other sphinx-supporting students, were huddled in the hallway. There were a few mathletes, an eighth grader on the debate team, the kid who was the petunia, a boy from the wrestling team, and a couple of others. "I was thinking we should call ourselves the Sphinx Squad." Nadia stopped. Everyone looked downcast. "Um, no worries," she said. "We can come up with another name."

"Sorry, Nadia," Vikram said. "It's not that." He handed her a piece of paper.

It was one of Nadia's Fun Sphinx Fact posters. Fun was crossed out and someone had written Nerd in its place.

"They're all like this," Chloe said. "I've been tearing them down when I see them."

Nadia's stomach did a flip. It was rough to see her hard work defaced like that. It made her think of a story she had found while doing her sphinx research about an ancient Egyptian couple whose tomb had been vandalized—their faces and names scratched out. Ancient Egyptians believed scratching out a name or image of someone had the power to harm or destroy them. On a (much) smaller scale, this felt the same.

"Want me to find who did this?" the wrestler asked. "I could make sure they don't do it again—"

"No!" Nadia said. "When they go low, we go high." That was one of her favorite Michelle Obama quotes. She took a deep breath. "We just need to up our game."

"Exactly!" Vikram said. "And I have an idea for that. Anyone who wants to hear it, grab your lunch and meet me behind the soccer field in ten. I want to keep this a surprise."

Chapter Twelve

Nadia and Adam headed to Titi's classroom at lunchtime the next day to fill him in on the no-longer-suspects.

"Mrs. Booker is out, too. Turns out she just loves anything ancient. So we're back to square *eno*," Adam finished.

"Pestilent papyrus, that's disappointing," Titi said. He brightened. "But we'll figure this out. I promise. Now, Nadia," Titi said, changing the subject. "Do you need any help with the mascot stuff? I saw what happened to your posters." He frowned. "I'm not sure exactly how much free time I have, but I could try to—"

"That's okay, Titi," Nadia said. There was no way she could ask for Titi's help now that he was fearing for his life. Besides, she had the Sphinx Squad.

She and Adam quickly told Titi about their mascot

plans. Vikram had been working on a sphinx costume. A boy named Sean who was in a band had taken it upon himself to record a song parody called "Who Let the Sphinx Out?" (It wouldn't have been Nadia's first choice for an anthem, but it was actually kind of catchy.) And Chloe had rounded up some kids who were going to perform a step routine and sphinx cheer. The Sphinx Squad was going to do a surprise performance in the cafeteria on Friday to show everyone that the sphinx was anything but nerdy.

They said goodbye and stepped into the hallway, almost bumping into Principal Taylor.

"Whoops. Excuse me, Adam, Nadia," he said, pushing past them into the classroom.

"Mr. Ferrari," they heard him say. "How would you like to start a history club . . ."

Nadia sighed. At this rate, even if they did catch Khefren, she'd never see Titi again. He was too busy being the most awesome teacher Bridget Mason had ever seen.

On Friday, when the bell rang for lunch, Nadia dashed to the bathroom and changed into jeans and a yellow shirt. The rest of the Sphinx Squad did the same. Nadia and Sarah grabbed the tote bag with the two long pieces of gold fabric they had borrowed from Mr. Ferrari (who else?). In just a few minutes, they were going to *be* the wings of the sphinx. After all the Khefren failures, Nadia really needed this to go well.

The Sphinx Squad gathered outside the cafeteria next to a newly hung hawk poster, trying to look as inconspicuous as possible, as kids made their way inside. This was particularly difficult for Vikram in his golden sphinx costume, which had turned out awesome.

"So, should we get started?" Sean asked. He had his portable speaker cued up to "Who Let the Sphinx Out?"

Nadia was about to say "go for it" when the fire alarm went off.

ERRRRRRNGH! ERRRRRRNGH! ERRRRRRNGH!

Everyone slapped their hands over their ears. Should they evacuate?

Principal Taylor pushed past the Sphinx Squad, standing in the cafeteria doorway as students started to flood out. "No need to panic, everyone!" he shouted. "False alarm! Just take your lunches outside to the quad until we can get the alarm turned off. It's a beautiful day. Nice breeze out there!"

The Sphinx Squad joined the flow of students headed outside.

"Now what?" Oona asked Vikram, shouting over the alarm. "Should we just wait till Monday?"

"Nah, let's do this," Vikram said (since the sphinx head isn't cover his whole head.).

Nadia smiled. Vikram was right. They wouldn't let a little change of venue stop them.

Once all the students from the cafeteria were settled in the quad, Adam took a couple steps back and began filming. He was hoping to get some footage for the newspaper.

"Here we go," said Vikram. "Sphinx Squad on three. One, two, three!"

"SPHINX SQUAD!" they all shouted. Vikram raced into the middle of the quad as Sean pressed play on the speaker.

Or did he?

"Can you turn the speaker up?" Nadia asked Sean.

Sean grimaced. "That's as loud as it goes. It's not really meant to be used outside like this."

Nadia motioned for Vikram to continue anyway. He ran around, trying to get everyone to cheer. Most people were confused, but a couple of kids clapped.

Vikram hammed it up, putting a paw to his giant sphinx head's ear. His message was clear. *I CAN'T HEAR YOU!*

Some kids whooped so loudly several other groups stopped eating to see what was going on.

That was Andrew's cue. He held up the megaphone. "Make some noise for the SPHIIIIINX SQUAAAAAAD!"

Chloe and her crew ran out to the middle of the quad and launched into a cheer. They clapped their hands and stomped their feet. Vikram continued riling up the crowd, making his way around the quad. More students put down their lunches to watch.

Nadia looked away from Vikram long enough to catch a glimpse of Mia and several other Hawkeyes staring at them. They did not look happy.

Vikram finished his circle around the quad and cartwheeled into the middle of Chloe's group (who knew Vikram could do cartwheels?!) just as they reached the last verse of the cheer. Nadia and Sarah ran out behind him, quickly attaching the fabric to his shoulders.

The crew formed a circle around Vikram, who was hamming it up big-time, and brought it home with the final cheer:

"You think you can outfight us?

Watch out for our claws.

You think you can outsmart us?

Our riddles get applause.

You think you can outrun us?

Well, think again, because . . ."

FWOOM!

Nadia and Sarah each took the end of their piece of the fabric and ran backward to unfurl it, creating the illusion of ten-foot wings behind Vikram. The crowd was silent for a moment, stunned at the gold fabric waving and sparkling in the sunlight.

Perfection, Nadia thought.

SWOOSH! A gust of wind tore the fabric from Nadia's hands and plastered it right across Vikram's face. Blinded, he stumbled back and knocked into Chloe, who fell into someone else . . . a classic domino effect.

The crowd roared with laughter.

A kid from the football team, clearly a Hawkeye, cupped his hands around his mouth and shouted, "I thought you Nerds were so smart! Can't handle a little wind, huh?"

The crowd laughed louder.

"What are you trying to say?" one of Chloe's crew called out, taking a step toward the football player.

No, no, Nadia thought. *When they go low, we go high!*

"You're not as smart as you think," the kid continued. "You act like you're so much better than us with your riddles and"—he looked right at Nadia—"your condescending newspaper articles. Yeah, I know big words, too!"

Nadia shook her head. "Nobody thinks that!" she shouted. But she felt a little needle of guilt because it was only last fall that she *did* think that. She grabbed the megaphone from Andrew and decided to be honest. "Truthfully, I did think that sports were stupid last semester, but then—"

"Stupid! She said she thinks sports are stupid!" someone yelled.

"Just let her finish!" Nadia heard Chloe shout.

SPLAT. Something hit the megaphone, then oozed off. Someone had thrown coleslaw at Nadia.

"FOOD FIGHT!" someone yelled.

Nadia ducked as cheeseburgers and French fries and pizza flew by.

THUNK. An apple hit Vikram's headpiece and spun it around backward.

"I can't see!" he cried.

"Get down!" Nadia yelled, dodging a spray of chocolate milk.

"Hey, Hawkeyes!" Nadia heard someone yell. "Hawks like to fly, but I bet they can't fly like this!" Nadia watched in horror as Oona—kind, polite Oona—launched a handful of Jell-O at a group of jocks. It hit an eighth grader square in the face.

"Huh," said Vikram. He'd taken off his headpiece. "Pretty good arm."

"Oh no you don't," a cheerleader shot back at Oona. She strode toward her, cafeteria tray in hand. "How about this riddle? What's yellow and goopy and looks like popcorn barf? Give up? Your face!" Then she dumped a bowl of creamed corn on top of Oona's head.

Nadia watched the terrible, ridiculous scene, her mouth open in shock. This whole mascot thing was supposed to bring the school together. How had it gone so wrong?

Chapter Thirteen

The magician was feeling pleased. Very pleased. Everything was proceeding according to plan. Soon it would be time to see things through to completion. And that teacher would be gone—forever. They said that revenge was a dish best served cold, and things were downright frigid after three thousand years.

And, best of all, his expensive nut addiction appeared to finally be over—the very thought of a pecan made him shudder.

"I'm telling you," Nadia said as she and Adam walked to school Monday morning. "It's just too much of a coincidence that someone pulled the fire alarm right before the Sphinx Squad was about to start. Someone must have tipped the Hawkeyes off and they pulled it to sabotage us."

"You think one of the Sphinx Squad spilled the beans?" Adam said. "That seems unlikely."

Nadia sighed. "I know. I was thinking more like the Hawkeyes were spying on us?"

But then again, Nadia was starting to think *everyone* was spying on them. They'd strategized about Khefren all weekend. She wondered if maybe they were going about it all wrong. What if Khefren wasn't someone on the school staff? What if he was a student? That was a whole lot of new possible suspects.

And she wasn't the only one who was getting paranoid. As they approached Main Street, the crossing guard hurried over to them. He held his stop sign aloft as he motioned for Nadia and Adam to follow him. Adam stopped in the middle of the street.

A car in the turning lane honked. The crossing guard turned around.

"Hurry along, son," he said.

"You started working here right after the holiday break, didn't you?" Adam asked him.

"Who, me?" asked the crossing guard.

"Yes, you," said Adam.

The car honked again. Nadia grabbed Adam's hand and pulled him toward the curb. The crossing guard followed behind them.

"I—I did," he said.

"And how exactly did you get the job?" Adam asked.

"Adam, that's enough," Nadia said through gritted teeth.

The crossing guard frowned. "When I found out that Mrs. Randazzo was taking a leave of absence, I asked her to recommend me for the job. And yes, I did bake her my famous chocolate chip cookies to thank her. But I swear it wasn't a bribe!"

"Of course it wasn't," said Nadia. She turned to Adam and pulled him down the sidewalk. "Great work there, Sherlock Holmes."

"I'm not apologizing," said Adam. "Until we find Khefren, everyone is a suspect."

Nadia sighed. She hoped they found Khefren soon. Then she could get back to everything else—the mascot contest, the paper . . .

Nadia did a face palm. *The paper.*

Their content for the second issue was due today. With all the Khefren strategizing, Nadia had completely forgotten to write her column!

"*Doog gninrom,*" Vikram said, catching up to Nadia and Adam on the school steps.

"But *is* it a good morning?" Adam said, looking puzzled. He pointed at Vikram's T-shirt. "That creature doesn't seem to think so."

Nadia glanced at Vikram's shirt. It had a photo of the oddest creature she had ever seen on it. It looked like a sack of gelatin with a huge bulbous nose, beady eyes, and a giant frown.

"The Blobster does indeed think it is a good morning," Vikram said. "Because he's going to keep the mascot contest civil this week." He pulled a stack of blobfish-shaped stickers from his backpack as they entered the main hallway of the school. The cartoon blobfish was cuter than the real one—hot pink with adorable little eyes and a raised eye-brow. It seemed to be saying "Hey there, pal!" rather than "Go away, please."

"Check it out," Vikram said. He found a sphinx poster on the wall. Nadia had put up new ones but most had already been defaced by Hawkeyes. This one now said "SPHINX NERD FACT: THEIR GREATEST FEAR IS A STRONG BREEZE."

SLAP. Vikram stuck a blobfish over the offending words. "The Blobster does not approve of slander. He may be considered ugly by some, but he does not tolerate ugly attitudes."

Nadia looked at the blobfish, then back at Vikram, then back at the blobfish. She burst out laughing.

"Vikram," she said, "You are so weird sometimes."

"Thank you," he replied.

Nadia spent the rest of the day trying to figure out her column. Ms. Tovey had not been happy when Nadia told her she hadn't finished it yet, but she said that as long as Nadia got her the article by 5 o'clock, she could drop it in the paper. If not, she'd have to give Nadia a zero for the assignment.

Titi had caught Nadia brainstorming column ideas during social studies.

He frowned when she explained her predicament. "Old Titi's a bit offended you haven't asked for his help."

"I know, Titi," Nadia had said. "But you have so much on your plate right now."

Titi softened. "I do have a pile of responsibilities taller than the pyramid of Giza," he said. "That's true. But I'm always in your corner, kid. You know that."

The final bell rang. Nadia headed to the computer lab. She sat there, staring at the screen.

"Nadia! There you are!" a voice called from the doorway.

"Oh no," Nadia grumbled. It was Ms. Tovey. Her teacher looked a little frantic as she scurried over.

"Mr. Taylor called an emergency staff meeting; I need your article by four o'clock now instead of five so I can get it to the printer before the meeting. Have you finished it?"

Nadia gulped. Finished? She hadn't even started.

Ms. Tovey softened when she saw the panic on Nadia's face. "Oh, Nadia," she said. "I know you were disappointed with your first column. Can I offer some advice? Take a risk! Step outside your comfort zone. Write something that will really grab students' attention. You're all about facts, which is great—you just have to find a way to jazz them up." She checked her watch.

"Already three fifteen! I've got a lot to do before the staff meeting." She hurried back down the hallway, calling to Nadia as she left. "I look forward to reading your column, Nadia. I know you can do it! And remember—"

"—check your sources," Nadia finished. That call and response had become a ritual in language arts class.

Nadia stared at the blank page. *Take a risk—that's definitely something Nellie Bly would do. But take a risk on what?* She still didn't even know what she was writing about.

She grabbed her water bottle and headed down the hallway to refill it. She was stalling, she knew, but she was pretty sure Nellie Bly would recommend a brisk walk to clear one's head when faced with writer's block.

Nadia glanced at the mascot posters as she walked. Vikram had stuck a blobfish on each one. Without warning, a ball of anger as intense as the Blobster's hot pink hue ignited in her chest. Because while the Blobster stickers were a creative way to help keep things civil, they shouldn't have been necessary in the first place.

After the food fight on Friday, Principal Taylor had told the whole school that while he was impressed with their "commitment to school spirit," he had expected more of his students. "I have always prided myself on Bridget Mason students showing respect and integrity in all their actions," he had said. Nadia had rolled her eyes. Because she had realized something: Their school was even more divided than she thought. Instead of bringing people together, it seemed to have given everyone an excuse to say out in the open the things they had apparently been saying behind each other's backs all along.

The sphinx was the opposite of all that. It was regal, it was smart, it was fierce. But now there were only two days until the final election and the sphinx's chances were looking worse than ever, all because the Hawkeyes had played dirty on Friday.

Nadia filled her water bottle and walked back to the computer lab.

A folder sat on her chair. There was a sticky note on the front:

Thought you might be able to use this.
—Titi

Nadia flipped opened the folder. Inside was a printout of an online article. She scanned it quickly and her eyes lit up. There was even a link to a video of an eyewitness account!

She sat down, quickly typed in the link, and watched the video, wincing. This would be the perfect topic for her column! She could even link to the video in her piece. *That* would grab everyone's attention.

And the timing could not be more perfect, with the paper coming out tomorrow morning and then the mascot vote happening during last period. Principal Taylor would be proud, too. Nadia would bring some integrity back to the election.

She started typing away, fingers clicking on the keys, her heart beating with excitement. Because this article was front-page worthy, yes, but also because Principal Taylor couldn't have been more wrong about Titi that day in the library. Even with everything on his plate, Titi had come through for her when it mattered.

Nadia was almost done writing when she remembered about checking sources. She had the website credibility checklist in her backpack. But she glanced at the clock—3:54 p.m.! There was no way she could check and add up all those points in time. Titi—a trusted teacher—had given her the information. What more reliable source did she need than that?

She did a quick read for any typos but didn't find any. This article was informative. It was different from what she'd normally write, but that's what Ms. Tovey had asked her to do. Sure, the column might upset some students, but sometimes the truth ruffled a few feathers. She giggled. Feathers!

She quickly wrote an email to Ms. Tovey, attached the article, and pressed send.

Her teacher responded back almost immediately. *Just in time, Nadia! I'm dropping it into the paper now!*

And Nadia was finally able to exhale. Whew!

Chapter Fourteen

Nadia sat down in homeroom, her eyes lighting up as soon as she saw the stack of newspapers on Ms. Arena's desk.

The teacher picked up a stack. "The second issue of *Newsflash* is here! Who wants to help me pass them out?"

Nadia raised her hand but the loudspeaker crackled to life. To her disappointment, Ms. Arena set the papers back down on her desk. *Thanks a lot, Principal Taylor*, she thought.

"Good morning, Bridget Mason Petunias, soon to be . . . whatever you decide!" The principal sounded breathless with excitement. "The final mascot vote is this afternoon! Now, at the suggestion of some wise sixth graders, we have improved the voting process since the primary."

Nadia smiled. The Nerd Patrol were those wise sixth graders. After the low turnout for the primary election, she'd suggested to Principal Taylor that they hand out ballots to the whole school and vote all at once, rather than requiring that students visit the main office on their own. Kids were busy with morning tutoring sessions, lunchtime homework clubs, after-school clubs, and detention. Voting in class would make sure everyone had a chance to make their voices heard.

"Voting will happen during last period. I will announce the results at the spirit rally tomorrow morning, and we will officially debut the new mascot at the Westside game next weekend. Good luck to both the sphinx and hawk! May the best mascot win!"

The loudspeaker clicked off, then right back on again.

"Oh! And I almost forgot, congratulations to class 605 on the second edition of *Newsflash*, which comes out today. I can't wait to read it! This is Principal Taylor. Over and out."

Ms. Arena began handing out the papers. Nadia smiled. Aside from the fact that they still had no clue who Khefren was, it was looking to be a very good day.

And it got even better when she saw that her story was on the front page!

Voting For The Hawk? Awk!

by Nadia Youssef

Sphinx vs. hawk. As every student at Bridget Mason Middle School knows, we will vote on a new mascot this afternoon. I nominated the sphinx. But I write to you today not as a member of the Sphinx Squad, but merely as a fellow student, concerned about our school's future.

The hawk is not fit to be our mascot.

It may be majestic. It may be fierce and fast.

But the hawk has a dark side: It has attempted to fly away with small children in its monstrous claws. If you access the link below, you will see a frightened mother, beating off a hawk trying to steal her small child.

Do we want our school to be represented by an animal capable of such terror? Do we want to give the impression that Bridget Mason students prey upon the innocent?

It is no riddle that our mascot should be—no, must be—the mighty sphinx.

And that's a fact.

Sarah turned around. "Wow, Nadia!"

Jason was seated behind her. "I had no idea that hawks did that. I admit I was maybe going to vote for the hawk—"

Nadia cut him off with a look.

"What?" Jason said. "The sphinx is awesome. But did you know that some hawks can go as fast as a hundred and fifty miles per hour when they dive? Totally cool, right?"

Nadia continued to stare.

"But—but it doesn't matter," Jason said. "Now I keep picturing my baby cousin getting snatched by one. Definitely gonna vote for the sphinx now."

"That's more like it," Nadia said, smiling.

Adam high-fived her. "Great job. Love the video link."

As Nadia and Adam made their way to math, she noticed that someone had torn down one of the hawk posters in the hallway.

Later, in language arts, Nadia and her classmates patted themselves on the back for a successful second issue, then started plotting out the next edition.

"I can write about the mascot results," Nadia offered.

"Oh, I wonder who's going to win now?" said Mateo with a laugh.

Nadia and Adam headed to their lockers at lunchtime. They passed Mr. Flores in the hallway.

"Hey, Mr. Flores!" Nadia said, waving.

Mr. Flores nodded, but didn't say anything.

"You know," Nadia said to Adam once they were out of earshot. "I've been trying to be extra nice to Mr. Flores ever since that litter pledge. But he never talks to me. I'm starting to think I did something to offend him."

Adam froze mid-step.

"You okay?" Nadia asked.

Instead of answering, Adam grabbed her arm and dragged her over to a copy of the No-Littering Pledge.

"The other day when I was waiting to get into science class after lunch, I saw the pledge and started to say it backward!"

"Of course you did," Nadia said, rolling her eyes.

"Wait," Adam says. "Listen—'I pledge.'" He said it more slowly. "'Pleh-dge.' Don't you hear it? 'Pleh' sounds like 'help' backward! Were you holding the amulet that day we did the trash pledge in language arts?"

Nadia thought back. "I was wearing the sweater your

122

mom gave me for Christmas. I was itchy and scratched my neck as I was reciting the pledge. My fingers must have touched the amulet." She shook her head. "So *that's* how Khefren got me to send Titi back into the amulet!"

"And now we know that Flores is Khefren!" Adam exclaimed.

"This is HUGE!" Nadia said. "But wait." She shook her head. "Nellie Bly would want more evidence. We have to make sure he's Mr. Flores."

"Well, let's go!" Adam said, ripping down the anti-littering pledge from the wall. "We can update Titi and make a plan."

Nadia's stomach growled. It looked like they were skipping actual lunch today. She grabbed an emergency granola bar from her backpack on the way to Titi's classroom.

When they got there, the classroom was set up like the Colosseum during one of the emperor's sea battle re-creations, with blue fabric for water and cardboard ships students could ride in. Nadia was impressed that Titi had planned such an interesting lesson in the midst of all this. She told him so.

"The show must go on!" Titi said with a shrug. "I am a teacher first. Always. But it looks like you two have something to report. What's the skinny?"

Five minutes later, Titi was up to speed on Flores.

"You know," Titi said, "I caught him swearing at me under his breath when he came to sweep my classroom the other day."

"See?" Adam said. "It's him!" He ran around the room. "We're gon-na catch Khef-ren! We're gon-na catch Khef-ren!"

"I hate to admit it, but that pledge is really clever," Titi continued. He thought for a moment. "Read that to me again?" As soon as Nadia read the words, "I pledge to do my duty," Titi stood up. "Holy hieroglyphs! Duty—that sounds a lot like . . ." He dropped his voice to a whisper. "Djehuty."

Adam stopped running. "Why are you whispering?" he asked.

"Because—" Titi paused. "You swear on a stack of papyrus that you won't tell a soul?"

"Cross my heart," Nadia said.

"And hope to die," Adam added.

"Well, that seems a little extreme," Titi said.

"Fine, I promise I won't tell," Adam said. "Now what does 'Djehuty' mean?"

"Djehuty is . . . " Titi lowered his voice so much that Nadia and Adam had to lean in to hear him. "My secret name."

"Looc," Adam whispered.

"Yeah, cool," Nadia added, whispering. "But, um, what's a secret name?"

Titi explained. In ancient Egypt, many children received a secret name at birth. No one knew it but them and the gods. Or in Titi's case, Titi, the gods, and Khefren. He had told his childhood best friend his secret name one day during an ancient Egyptian equivalent of Truth or Dare.

"So?" Adam said after Titi had finished. "What's the

big deal with a word sounding like your secret name being in the pledge? Are you embarrassed because it sounds like 'doody'? I can beat you on that one. I don't tell many people my middle name—but Nadia knows it, right?"

"I do indeed, Adam Leprechaun," Nadia said with a little giggle.

"My birthday is Saint Patrick's Day," Adam explained to Titi.

But Titi didn't so much as crack a smile. "It's a big deal because I'll bet you anything that 'duty' was in the pledge to make sure I got sent back to the amulet and not Khefren, too. Secret names were very powerful in ancient Egypt. If someone had yours, they could basically control you. Hence the whole secret thing."

"Oh." Nadia sat down. "That is serious."

"So you're saying we need Khefren's secret name if we want to get him back in the amulet?" Adam asked.

"Uh-huh. If we want him to go back and not me," Titi said. He was pacing now.

Nadia smiled. "But surely if you told him your secret name, then he must have told you his?"

Titi jumped onto his desk and went into meditation mode. Nadia and Adam stared, not wanting to disturb him. The minutes ticked by. Nadia finished her granola bar, and a second one, too. Finally, with two minutes until the end-of-lunch bell, Titi's eyes snapped open. "*Sa!*"

"*Sa?!*" said Nadia and Adam together.

Titi nodded. "It's the ancient word for 'pig.'"

125

Fun Fact: According to ancient Egyptian myth, the goddess Isis tricked the god Ra into giving her his secret name.

Nadia giggled. "*Sa*" made this evil magician they were so afraid of seem a little less intimidating.

"Well, quick!" said Adam said to Nadia. "Unwrap the amulet and send him back!"

"Yes!" Titi said. "We'll be done with all this before class starts!"

Nadia grabbed the amulet and furiously unwrapped the yarn. She held the amulet aloft and took a deep breath.

"Wait," she said, bringing the amulet back down. "This won't work. Or rather, it might work, but we won't know that it worked. When I sent Titi back to the amulet with the pledge, I had no idea it had happened. It wasn't until I accidentally released him and saw him in my notebook that I realized, remember?" She shook her head. "We need to do this in front of Khefren, so we can know for sure that he actually goes back."

"Blustering beetles, you're right," said Titi.

Flores always emptied Titi's trash at the end of the day. They agreed to meet in his classroom after school.

Nadia practically skipped off to PE. Her article was a hit, and they were this close to finding Khefren. This was turning out to be a most excellent day.

Nadia's elation lasted until she was on her way to fifth period and someone knocked into her in the hallway. She looked up and found herself face-to-face with Mia.

"You're going to pay for this, Youssef," Mia said, holding up the newspaper. "I know this whole mascot contest was your idea and obviously you want the sphinx to win, but

I honestly didn't think you were capable of something this low. I called my dad and he's talking with Principal Taylor right now." She stormed off.

Low?! Nadia thought. *Low is sabotaging the Sphinx Squad's lunchtime show!* Her article had simply told the truth. Students deserved to know the facts about the mascot they were voting for.

Ten minutes later, science class was interrupted when the loudspeaker began to hiss and hum. "Attention, students. This is Principal Taylor. This morning I saw you all in the hallways enjoying the new issue of *Newsflash*. Unfortunately, I have received some very disturbing information: That article about the hawk is fake news."

Nadia froze. *Fake news?*

"I will be conducting an investigation to determine whether this false information was distributed accidentally or intentionally. In the meantime, please rest assured that hawks do not and cannot steal small children. The mascot election will continue as planned this afternoon. But I ask that you do your best to not let today's media mayhem inform how you vote. That's all, students," Principal Taylor finished. "Ms. Tovey and Nadia Youssef, please report to my office immediately."

The entire class swiveled around to stare at Nadia. She gulped.

So much for an excellent day.

Chapter Fifteen

I swear, I didn't know it was fake," Nadia said to Principal Taylor and Ms. Tovey. "Someone left a folder on my chair in the computer lab with an article about hawks inside. Maybe it was supposed to be a joke or something."

On the way to Taylor's office, Nadia had done a quick search on her phone: "hawk stealing baby video real?" Her stomach had dropped when she saw the results: FALSE. Hawks do not steal children. Then, just to see how clueless she was, she ran through Mrs. Booker's website credibility list on the website Titi's article had come from. The site got negative points. Nadia didn't know that was possible.

How could she have been so careless? It would have

taken twenty seconds to do that same search before she hit send yesterday. But here she was.

Taylor narrowed his eyes, considering Nadia's explanation. "Publishing false information does seem out of character for you, Nadia. You're usually so careful with your facts. Didn't Ms. Tovey teach you to verify your sources?"

"Yes, she did," Nadia said, hanging her head. "And I—"

"Principal Taylor," Ms. Tovey suddenly said. "Before we go any further, I have to be completely honest—I didn't actually read Nadia's article before putting it in the paper."

"What?" Nadia said. "But you—"

"I'm sorry, Nadia," Ms. Tovey said. "You're always such a good student—so on top of your game. And I had to attend your emergency staff meeting, Mr. Taylor. I just didn't have time to read it. But that's no excuse. I should have. I'm sorry."

"Thank you for sharing that," Principal Taylor said to Ms. Tovey. Then he quickly turned his attention back to Nadia. "Your article was especially shocking knowing that the sphinx of ancient Greece had a proclivity to consume those who couldn't answer her riddles. Talk about the pot calling the kettle black." He clicked his tongue. "Not a good look, Nadia."

Nadia sank down in her seat. Seemed she'd conveniently forgotten that part. Now she was a hypocrite, on top of everything else.

"But my biggest concern is still that you spread a lie about the hawk," Principal Taylor said.

Nadia took a deep breath and sat up straight. "But I didn't know it was a lie. A friend gave me a printout and maybe they didn't know—"

"Hmmmm. Is this the same friend who's been flaky lately?" Principal Taylor asked.

Nadia just stared at him, not even wanting to think about what he was implying.

"Well, I can't speak for you, Nadia," Principal Taylor said, "but intentionally or not, this friend put you in an awful situation. If it were me, I would get this toxic person out of my life for good."

Nadia stared down at her hands, a million thoughts running through her head.

"I'm sorry this happened to you," Principal Taylor said. "And I wish I didn't have to do what I'm about to do . . . I'm going to let the mascot election continue, but I'm afraid I have to end *Newsflash* early."

"But Mr. Taylor—" Ms. Tovey started to protest.

Principal Taylor held up a hand to silence her.

"You can punish me," Nadia said. "I deserve it. But please don't make my classmates suffer because of something I did."

"It must be done," said Principal Taylor. "This sends the message that we take journalistic integrity very seriously here at Bridget Mason Middle School."

Nadia turned to Ms. Tovey. Surely she could help. But her teacher just shook her head. "I'm sorry, Nadia. It sounds like 605's newspaper time is done."

Nadia managed a small nod, then stormed out of Principal Taylor's office and down the hallway.

"Hey, there goes Fake News Nadia!" a kid called out.

Nadia shot him a look but kept going. She ran to the girls' bathroom, locked herself in a stall, and let the tears fall.

She would be the laughing stock of the school. Her class would never forgive her for getting *Newsflash* shut down. And the sphinx was definitely not going to win the mascot contest now.

Taylor's words came back to her: *Intentionally or not, this friend put you in an awful situation.*

But Titi couldn't have given her false information accidentally—he was the smartest person she knew.

Nadia let out a sob, because that left her to conclude one thing: Titi had set her up. But why would he do such a thing?

She paused, tissue midway to her face. That was just it—Titi wouldn't do anything to hurt her, but she knew someone who would.

She raced out of the bathroom.

"Nadia!" Adam said, catching up to her in the hallway. "What did Taylor say?"

Nadia ignored him. She pulled the folder from the computer lab out of her backpack and burst into Titi's classroom without even knocking, Adam right on her heels. Titi was sitting on one of the marble pedestals, meditating.

"Have you ever seen this folder before?" She held it up in front of Titi's face.

Titi's eyes flew open and he fell off the pedestal with a thud. "Heavens to Hatshepsut, Nadia! A little warning next time?"

"This," Nadia said, pointing to the sticky note. "Did you write it?"

Titi peered at the note. "I did not. But what an excellent forgery!"

"Exactly!" Nadia said, tossing the folder down on Titi's desk. "I've been set up!" She started pacing, and filled them in on the folder, the article, and her meeting with Principal Taylor and Ms. Tovey. "So not only am I now 'Fake News Nadia,' but they're shutting down *Newsflash*, all because you"—she pointed at Titi—"supposedly left me this folder. And if I didn't trust you as much as I do, setting me up like that might make me angry with you. Angry enough to . . ."

Titi's eyes went wide. "Send me back to the amulet! You think Khefren left that folder for you?"

"Whoa," Adam said. "I think I get it." He scrunched up his face, thinking. "Khefren needs Titi back in the amulet. You're the only one who can send him there. Khefren already tried getting you to send Titi back accidentally, but that didn't work . . . the only foolproof way to get Titi back in the amulet—and have him stay there—would be to get you angry enough to send him back on purpose. Is that right?"

Nadia nodded.

"That sounds like Khefren all right," Titi said. "Suffering sarcophagi, we need to start investigating on Flores, stat."

Adam lifted his chin. "Well, whether Flores really is Khefren, you didn't fall for Khefren's tricks, Nadia. If he wants you out of his life for good, he's going to have to try harder than that."

Nadia's blood froze.

Out of my life for good. Where had she heard that before?

She gasped. It suddenly all made sense.

The pledge. The pressure for Titi to start a magic club and a history club, which meant he'd have less time for her. Her conversation with Taylor in the library. The fire alarm. The emergency staff meeting, which made sure Tovey didn't have time to review her article. And finally, her conversation with Principal Taylor in his office just now.

"Flores isn't Khefren!" she shouted. "Taylor is!"

Chapter Sixteen

Nadia could hear the roar of students in the gym. It was first thing Wednesday morning and she, Adam, and Titi were in Titi's classroom, which was all set up for his next lesson on Neptune, the Roman god of the sea. Titi had changed the lightbulbs to blue for an underwater feel; placed plastic sea creatures around the classroom; and hung a giant fishing net from the ceiling. Perhaps most impressively, he had created a gigantic sparkly coral reef. Nadia was pretty sure he'd used an industrial-sized vat of glitter.

Nadia glanced out the door and saw a fifth grader scurrying down the hall so he wouldn't be late to the spirit rally. She had voted for the mascot, along with everyone else, in last period the previous afternoon. It had felt like all eyes were on her as she filled the ballot out. She had double-checked it before submitting it. She had been so distracted by the realization that Taylor was Khefren that she wouldn't have put it past herself to have marked the wrong box.

But now, while the entire school attended the rally, Nadia, Adam, and Titi would be proving in all certainty that Taylor was Khefren. And then they'd be getting rid of him for good.

Nadia did a mental check that they had everything they needed. *Hippo amulet—check! Adam's voice recorder—check! Nadia's notebook—check! Khefren's secret name—check!*

Nadia's stomach flipped. The first part of their plan was for safety. To keep the real Principal Taylor out of harm's way, they needed to get Khefren to leave the principal's body.

Adam poked his head out the door. "Taylor's coming down the hallway!" he whispered.

Nadia put her hands deep in her pockets. She couldn't risk touching the now-sweaterless hippo for this first part.

"THAT'S IT!" she yelled at Titi, loud enough for Taylor to hear. "YOU RUINED MY REPUTATION AND NOW *NEWSFLASH* IS CANCELED. I'M DONE WITH YOU!"

"BUT NADIA—" Titi shouted back.

"BUT NOTHING! I PLEDGE TO DO MY DUTY AND PUT MY TRASH—INCLUDING YOU—WHERE IT BELONGS," she said.

Magical words now safely over, Nadia took her hands out of her pockets, grabbed the amulet, and tossed it into the metal garbage can, where it clanged loudly. Then she and Adam stormed out of the room and hid behind a row of lockers while Titi poofed onto some papers scattered on his desk.

As soon as they left, Principal Taylor emerged from the shadows and ducked into the classroom. He'd taken the bait! Nadia and Adam snuck up to the door and peered inside.

Taylor hastily retrieved the amulet from the trash, a sly grin on his face, and placed it on Titi's desk—not far from where the animated Titi was holding a pose. Then he stepped back and thrust a hand out toward the amulet. It was the least-Taylor-like pose ever, full of arrogance. If there was any question that Taylor was actually Khefren, here was the answer.

The hairs on the back of Nadia's neck stood up. Things were getting *real*.

"Part Two, go!" Nadia whispered.

Adam nodded and started his voice recorder.

Taylor began chanting some ancient words, presumably the spell that would destroy the amulet forever. Purple smoke, then sparks began to form around his hand. While he was distracted, animated Titi crept across the paper until he was right under the amulet.

Just before Taylor finished his destroy spell, Titi poofed back to human form and grabbed the hippo.

Adam pressed stop on the recorder, then played the recording backward at full volume. Titi recited the backward words out loud as Taylor sneered and threw the purple sparks at the hippo.

Time seemed to slow as Nadia watched the purple

sparks bounce off the amulet and head back toward Taylor. Titi saying the spell backward had reversed its direction!

The principal's mouth fell open, then his body crumpled to the ground as Khefren exited it to dodge the destroy spell.

SPPPTTTTTTT! The purple sparks hit Titi's coral reef and it flew apart in a magnificent explosion of glitter.

Nadia and Adam ran to Titi's side shouting excitedly as glitter rained down around them. Part Two had worked!

But where was Khefren? Nadia's heart beat faster.

"Clever, very clever," a voice said.

Nadia whipped around as the magician stepped out from behind a pillar. He was absurdly tall and thin. His lavender eyes might have been pretty if not for the menacing glint in them. He wore so much gold jewelry that the morning sun lit him up like he was practically on fire.

She climbed up onto a nearby chair and Titi tossed her the amulet. Her heart was beating so hard now, she was sure the kids in the gym could hear it.

She held the amulet aloft. This was it.

"Pleh Sa!" she shouted. Then she braced for Khefren to disappear into the hippo.

But other than an evil grin creeping onto Khefren's face, nothing happened.

She gave Titi a panicked glance, but he looked as confused as she felt.

Khefren broke the silence with a loud cackle. "People change. You would agree, wouldn't you, Titi?"

Titi gave him a quizzical look.

"The secret name I was given at birth didn't really suit the powerful magician I had become." Khefren said. He shrugged. "So I changed it."

Nadia's blood boiled. Khefren was so arrogant, he had changed the name the gods had given him? What were they going to do now? She glanced from Adam to Titi.

Titi let out a nervous laugh, then extended his arms out to give Khefren a hug—a desperate attempt to shift the mood. "Khefren! Old buddy, old pal! It's been a while!"

"Oh, stop it," Khefren said. "You're pathetic." He took a step toward Nadia, who was still standing on the chair. "You are a smart girl, Nadia. You don't need this fool." He took another step forward. "It's time to send him back into the amulet. Now."

Nadia put her hands on her hips. "No," she said simply.

"Maybe you didn't hear me," Khefren said, taking another step closer. They were eye-to-eye now. "I said SEND HIM BACK."

"Maybe you didn't hear me," Nadia replied, stepping from the chair onto a desk. "I said NO!"

Khefren let out a howl, not unlike Nadia's toddler cousin did when throwing a tantrum, and began pacing around the room.

"Desperate much, Khefren?" Titi said mockingly.

"Stupid much, Titi?" Khefren replied, gaining back some composure. "Your jokes are what got us into this mess in the first place."

"We both know that's not true," Titi said.

"You may be a teacher, but you never seem to learn!" shouted Khefren. "I'm the real magician. I have all the power." He pulled back his hand, gathering red smoke and sparks, and threw them toward Titi. The sparks bounced off him, hitting a gigantic seahorse and shattering it.

Titi laughed. "You know you can't hurt me," he said to Khefren. "What, you enjoy casting spells for fun?"

Khefren pointed to Nadia. "Fine. I may not be able to hurt you, but she's mortal."

Nadia held up the amulet. "Really? Without me, this hippo is just a pretty necklace." Her hand shook a bit as she held the amulet aloft, but her voice was clear and steady.

Khefren spun around and pointed to Adam, pulling back his arm. "Well, how about your little redheaded friend?"

"Run, Adam!" Titi shouted.

Titi dove to block the green and yellow sparks that flew from Khefren's hand toward Adam. Adam hightailed it out of the classroom.

Khefren took off for the door. "Send Titi back and I won't harm your friend!" he shouted. Then he threw electric blue sparks at the gigantic fish net hanging above. It landed on Nadia and Titi as Khefren disappeared down the hallway.

They untangled themselves quickly, but Khefren's ruse had worked. By the time they entered the hallway, Khefren— and Adam—were nowhere to be seen.

They raced to the end of the corridor and saw a flash of Khefren's tunic as he turned the next corner.

"Come on!" Titi said, still running. "I'll see if I can slow him down."

POOF! They rounded the corner just in time to see a pizza costume appear over Khefren's tunic.

"For Adam," Titi said.

Nadia giggled as Khefren stumbled, the narrow bottom of the costume tripping him.

But her giggles faded when she saw that Khefren had Adam trapped in a corner. Her friend looked positively terrified. A cheerful bake sale poster, covered in drawings of cupcakes with big eyes and toothy grins, hung above his head, as if mocking him.

Nadia turned to Titi, her eyes filled with tears. "Do something!" she said.

Pizza-Khefren, one hand poised to blast a spell at Adam,

grinned. "You think his amateur magic is any match for mine, girl? Now repeat after me. 'I pledge to do my duty—'"

"Hang on to your hats!" shouted Titi.

POOF! Suddenly, Nadia, Titi, and Adam were tiny animated versions of themselves, standing on the bake sale poster. "Eat us! Eat us!" the cupcakes cried, jumping up and down.

Khefren was looking around wildly, trying to figure out where they had disappeared to.

A cupcake pulled on the hem of Nadia's sweater. "We're yummy! Put us in your tummy!" Nadia took a step back— the cupcake's voice was creepy. "Put us in your tummy! We'll make you feel crummy!"

"Yikes!" Titi cried. "Khefren went that way. We can't let him get near the spirit rally in the gym." He jumped from the bake sale poster to a book fair sign. Adam and Nadia followed, but they were promptly chased by a bunch of Goosebumps books (and there were many of them), their pages flapping.

"Sacrificial sassafras!" said Titi. "Khefren's bad magic must be making everything go cuckoo!"

"I don't want to get a paper cut!" Adam yelled.

They hopped to another bake sale poster, then a sphinx poster. "Aha!" cried the sphinx. "You can go no farther until you answer my riddle. What has four legs in the morning—"

"Humans!" said Nadia, cutting the sphinx off as they ran across the page.

"Oh snap," said the sphinx.

Titi, Nadia, and Adam raced from poster to poster. Band practice sign-up sheets with angry instruments and signs for lost retainers ("Now this is the height of grossness," said Adam as they dodged an irate retainer the same size as them). They were almost stomped on by sneakers on a walkathon banner, but leapt onto a Teacher Appreciation Day poster just in time.

"There you are," said the cartoon teacher. "Where is your homework?"

"Uh, my evil magician ate it," Nadia said as they jumped to a copy of the No-Littering Pledge.

They skidded to a stop when they saw Pizza-Khefren at the end of the hallway. He was standing right outside the closed gym doors. Nadia could hear shouts from the spirit rally.

Adam was glancing at the wall ahead of them. "We're out of posters!"

It was true. The corridor to the gym was cinder block. Tape didn't stick, so no one ever hung posters there.

"All those innocent students in the gym," Nadia said, panic in her voice. "He'll destroy them!"

Titi quickly cast a spell. POOF! A huge lock and chain appeared on the gym door. Then POOF!, Titi poofed them back into their human forms.

"I don't quite have a plan yet, "Titi said, "but I will by the time we get there."

They crept up behind Khefren.

"What's he doing?" Adam whispered as they got closer.

"I don't like the look of this . . ." Titi said.

All of a sudden, Khefren's head began to grow inside the pizza costume until it burst the seams. A bumpy green head and long snout appeared.

Titi's eyes went wide. "Uh-oh. I knew Khefren was a powerful magician but I didn't know he could shape-shift."

"Sh-shape-shift?" Adam stammered.

Khefren turned his head to the side. Rows of sharp pointy teeth appeared in his massive jaw. Then his body began to grow as his arms and legs shrank. Khefren was morphing into a crocodile!

Croc-Khefren, his metamorphosis complete, rammed into the doors with his massive body. The lock broke like it was made of cheap plastic.

Then Croc-Khefren slithered into the gym.

Chapter Seventeen

Nadia, Adam, and Titi ran after him but were greeted by a wall of students pushing and shoving one another. Nadia hadn't been to many spirit rallies, but she was pretty sure this wasn't normal. And where was Croc-Khefren?

Vikram ran up to them. "Nadia! Adam! Where have you been? The crowd got restless waiting for Principal Taylor to show up with the mascot results. I mean, how many times can you listen to the marching band play the school song? Oh, and get this—rumor has it that Mia didn't even want to nominate the hawk—Taylor said she'd get out of detention if she nominated it and no more detentions for the year if it won. Weird, right? Anyway, then someone yelled 'The Sphinx stinks!' and someone else yelled 'The Hawk is awk!' and a kid dressed up like the hawk shoved a kid in a sphinx costume and then everyone went wild, rushing the floor and pushing and yell—"

"Thanks for the recap, Vikram," Titi said, standing on tiptoes, trying to look over the crowd for Khefren. "Now if you'll excuse me, I'm, uh, I'm about to, uh, do a special magic show for everyone."

As if on cue, a stream of purple and orange sparks shot up toward the ceiling from the center of the gym. It hit a metal pipe with a loud clang and sparks rained down.

Fun Fact: The ancient Egyptians worshipped Sobek, a crocodile god. His temple was in a city called "Crocodilopolis."

Khefren!

All over the gym, confused students stopped shoving and yelling. They stared at the sparkle-producing creature that had just appeared in their gymnasium, waiting to see what would happen next.

Titi seized the opportunity. "Students!" he yelled. "Please back away from the crocodile. He's part of my exciting new magic show!"

The crowd obeyed, forming a large circle several people deep. Nadia, Adam, and Titi stood on the inner edge, not taking their eyes off Croc-Khefren. He pushed up to stand on his hind legs, his little arms crossed, as if he was amused to see how it was all going to play out.

Then someone started clapping. "Yeah, Mr. Ferrari! Show us some magic!" they shouted.

"You want to see magic?" Croc-Khefren growled at the crowd. "I'll show you magic!" And before everyone's unbelieving eyes he began to grow, until his head almost touched the gymnasium ceiling.

"GRRRRRRR!" he roared, ripping down several championship banners that hung from the ceiling.

The crowd gasped, but several people laughed, too.

"Is this our new mascot?" Nadia heard someone ask. She gulped. How long until everyone realized how much danger they were all in?

Croc-Khefren dropped to his belly with a huge thud. He flicked his giant tail toward a group of cheerleaders. They dodged him in a flurry of toe-touch jumps.

The crowd oohed and aahed—they were loving this "magic show."

Khefren picked up a gym mat in his giant pointy teeth and shook it. Stuffing flew everywhere and the crowd roared with laughter. Nadia gulped again as she imagined a kid in place of the gym mat. Or what was left of the mat.

"Nadia, Adam," Titi said, as Croc-Khefren blew teal smoke out his nostrils. Nadia did not like the look of that. Was fire next?

"I have a feeling this isn't going to be over until Khefren and I exchange three thousand years' worth of words," Titi said. "We can still capture him, Nadia. We'll get the new secret name out of him, I promise. When I think there's something that might be his name, I'll do this—" He ran his hand through his hair—or what would be his hair if he had any—in a classic Elvis Presley move. "Adam, you look up the ancient word for it on your phone, then Nadia, try that word in the hippo spell. Say it low—it'll keep us ahead of him. Sound good?"

Nadia and Adam nodded.

"And I'm going to keep your classmates safe, don't worry," Titi said. "Now watch out—Titi's about to go turbo!"

He turned around to face Khefren, hands on his hips.

"What's the matter, Khefren?" Titi shouted at the crocodile. "You're afraid to face me in regular old human form? Oh, that's right. You never could handle being my equal. Had to tear me—and everyone else—down every chance you got. You know what they call that, Khefren? A coward. Or in your case, a croc-coward-ile." Titi laughed at his own word play as he ran a hand over his head.

Adam typed away. "The ancient word for crocodile is 'mish,'" he said a moment later.

Nadia said, "*pleh mish.*"

But instead of disappearing, Khefren's skin began to change and his body began to shrink as the crowd gasped. This was the most amazing magic show any of them had ever seen! In just a few seconds, he was human Khefren again. The amulet spell hadn't worked, but at least Titi's taunts had some effect!

"Fine!" Khefren shouted in his regular voice again. "You happy now? Is that what you want? To see my face as I destroy your beloved students? I don't discriminate, you know. They're all fair game. Until Nadia sends you back, I won't stop." With a dramatic flourish, he threw pink sparks at the heads of a few students.

Titi thought fast and POOF! POOF! POOF! Each of those students' heads was covered in a helmet—a football helmet, a gladiator helmet, and an astronaut helmet, to be precise. Khefren's spells bounced off them. The crowd cheered.

Nadia clutched the amulet in her hand, terrified. *Another name! We need another name!*

"Ah, but you lie, Khefren!" Titi shouted. He and Khefren were circling each other now, staring each other down. "You did discriminate. Always. You decided who you liked and didn't like, and it was never based on merit, or integrity, or anything honorable. You only liked people you could use to gain power." He ran his hand over his head. "And when you were done with them, you tossed them away!"

"The ancient word for power is 'phety,'" Adam said.

"Pleh phety," Nadia said. Nothing.

"You mean like how I threw you away?" Khefren shouted at Titi, laughing. "Is old Titi still mad his BFF didn't want to be his friend anymore?" He sent a handful of purple sparks toward Titi.

Titi launched into a backflip to dodge the spell and it went flying past . . . straight toward Ms. Tovey.

POOF! A garden's worth of rosebushes sprang up in front of her. The spell hit them and a shower of fragrant petals rained down on everyone. The crowd cheered again.

Titi turned back to Khefren. "You lie again!" Titi shouted. "You were a horrible leader"—he ran his hand over his head—"and a horrible friend, too. It was me who left you, remember?"

"Oh, I remember," Khefren said to Titi. "The day you left was one of the best of my life."

Ouch, Nadia thought. That had to sting.

"'Leader' is 'seshemu,'" Adam said.

"Pleh seshemu," Nadia said. Still nothing.

Khefren threw more spells at random students, one after the other. POOF! POOF! POOF! POOF! Each student was suddenly clad in protective gear from head to toe. A fireproof jumpsuit. A suit of armor. Bubble wrap. And an Elvis costume with enough rhinestones to form a protective shield.

Khefren threw a few more spells, and Titi blocked each one, but, Titi seemed to be getting tired. Or maybe Khefren's last comment had thrown him off. A giant turtle shell appeared on the last student. She ducked inside, but her hair got singed.

The crowd yelped.

Nadia's stomach flipped. They had to figure out how to stop Khefren—fast. She glanced at Titi.

Khefren let out a maniacal laugh. "There's nothing you can do without my secret name. That amulet is useless without it." He shook his head. "And I'm getting bored."

He started making big circles with his arms, faster and faster. There was an unsettling humming sound, and all of a sudden there was a huge collective gasp from the students, teachers, and faculty as they shot up off the ground toward the ceiling. Nadia, Titi, and Khefren were left standing alone in the middle of the gym.

The kids screamed.

"What's happening?"

"I'm afraid of heights!"

Nadia gulped. This was bad. Very, very bad.

"It's simple, Nadia!" Khefren shouted. "Get rid of Titi and I won't let your friends fall forty feet." He smiled cruelly at Titi. "And don't bother trying anything. Your magic is child's play."

Titi and Khefren began shouting at each other—something about who won a papyrus boat race and Titi helping Khefren out with a school exam but Khefren never thanking him. Then Titi abandoned his Elvis move and began simply shouting out ancient words that Nadia quickly copied in the spell. Khefren stood there, arms crossed, saying "wrong" to each one and throwing sparks at Titi, who was starting to look desperate.

Bzzzz. Nadia's phone vibrated in her pocket. She ignored it.

Bzzzzz. Bzzzzz. Bzzzzz. Bzzzzz.

Something told Nadia she should look.

The texts were from Adam:

I'm up here next to Mia.

Mia said it's true—Taylor told her to nominate the hawk. Is Taylor's secret name the ancient word for HAWK?! I'm looking it up. Hold on . . .

Nadia's heart beat faster. That was almost too easy. But it did make sense. Hawks were revered in ancient Egypt—there was even an all-powerful, hawk-headed god named Horus. Khefren probably thought he deserved to be worshipped. It was worth a try.

Bzzzz. Adam sent her the ancient word but before she could look, her phone was ripped from her hands by an unseen force.

"You preteens and your phones!" Khefren thundered. "Such a distraction! And the screaming!" He glanced above. "I can't hear myself think!" With a wave of his hand, everyone above went silent.

Nadia's stomach turned as her friends noiselessly screamed above her. Titi's illusion of "this is all a magic show" would surely crumble now.

Khefren aimed a hand toward the ceiling, his focus still on Nadia. "Put him in the amulet NOW, girl, or I drop your friends."

Nadia glanced from her friends above to Titi. There was no way to ask Titi for the word for *hawk* without putting her classmates in danger. What was she going to do?

Titi looked at Nadia and smiled sadly.

"It's time, Nadia," he said. "I'm so sorry. You can send me back. It's okay, really."

Nadia choked back tears. What would she do without him? She hung her head.

There, on the ground by her feet, was a mascot mask covered in feathers. The hawk. And it came to her, sudden and crystal clear. She didn't need the *word* for hawk—all she needed was an image. Names in ancient Egypt *were* images—hieroglyphs. She remembered that story she'd found in her sphinx research—how those people erased their enemies' memory by scratching out their names on their tomb. Maybe, just maybe, the same would work here.

"I'm sorry, Titi," she said, to throw Khefren off.

"Don't be," Titi replied.

Nadia held the amulet aloft. Then she jumped in the air. Just as she landed on the hawk head, she shouted "PLEH!" The papier-mâché mask shattered, sending feathers flying. She had a sudden inspiration and added: "*Ye nih*—I mean, *you need* never come back!"

"Noooooooo!" Khefren began to shriek. Then SHWOOOOP! he disappeared into the amulet.

Nadia stared at the purple smoke left floating in the air, her mouth open in shock. Had that really just happened?!

A second later, her knees buckled and she collapsed onto the floor.

Titi raced over and crouched down. "You did it! How did you figure out—"

"That was all Adam," Nadia said, trying to catch her breath. "But yeah, we did it!" She started to get up, but suddenly remembered that everyone was still floating high above them. "Any ideas?" she said to Titi, pointing to the ceiling.

Titi stood back up. "I have just the thing."

POOF! He released Khefren's spell and everyone began to slowly sink, first quietly, then more loudly as they realized their voices were back, too.

Titi paused a moment, then flicked a finger at the students. POOF! Everyone in the gym, including Nadia, was holding a stick of fluffy cotton candy (blue, of course).

"Ooo! Nice touch!" Nadia said, grabbing a piece to stuff in her mouth.

"Jumping jackals!" Titi said, slapping her hand away. "Sorry about that—I shouldn't have given you any, Nadia. That delectable delight is filled with memory-erasing magic. Once everyone has a taste, all they'll recall from today is that they saw a really amazing magic show at the spirt rally. But you"—he extended a hand to help Nadia up—"You should remember this victory. Tell Adam not to eat any either, okay?"

Nadia grabbed Titi's hand and jumped up just as her

friends floated down around her. "You got it, Ti—I mean, Mr. Ferrari."

Chloe came running over to them, her mouth blue.

"Mr. Ferrari—that show was AMAZING!" she cried. "How did you—"

Tweeeeeeeeeeeeeeeeeeeeeeeee!!! An ear-deafening whistle filled the gym.

Everyone turned to see where the noise had come from.

And there, at the top of the bleachers, stood Principal Taylor—the real one—with a whistle in his mouth. He was wearing his green spandex Petunia mascot costume straight out of 1984, giant pink petals surrounding his face.

Chapter Eighteen

Nadia?" Sarah said at lunch the following day. "Are you okay? Would some chocolate pudding cheer you up?"

Nadia shook her head. She hadn't touched her hawawshi, either. And it was one of her favorites.

After Principal Taylor had blown his whistle at the pep rally yesterday, he made everyone take a seat in the bleachers. And the words he said next were a real blow: He was calling off the mascot contest.

Nadia's heart had sunk. Sure, she defeated an evil magician and saved Titi's life. Rescued her classmates, too. But she was also responsible for getting Newsflash canceled, and now, it seemed, the mascot contest, too.

Principal Taylor had said he never should have agreed to it in the first place. What was wrong with the petunia? What happened to school tradition? And clearly the students couldn't be trusted with such a large decision as choosing a new mascot. He looked around the gym. "Look at this mess!" he shouted. "The school board is going to have my hide!"

Nadia had noted that poor Principal Taylor sounded more than a little confused. She wondered what he remembered from the last few weeks.

She stopped by his office after school. She imagined asking him, "So do you have any memory of your body being possessed by an ancient magician with anger issues?"

But instead she said, "What about *Newsflash*? Could 605 finish it? Please?"

Principal Taylor sighed. "I feel like I want to say yes—"

Nadia's heart leapt with joy.

"—but the truth is . . ." He lowered his voice. "I can't remember why I shut it down in the first place. Refresh my memory?"

"We had a . . . misunderstanding," Nadia said. "About fake news. It wasn't all my fault . . . but some of it was."

Nadia had been thinking about that a lot. So a maniacal magician had manipulated her into making a choice about the hawk article. But it had been *her* choice to not verify that website.

Principal Taylor had thought for a long minute. Finally, he shook his head. "I've already changed my mind about the mascot," he said. "I've got to stick with at least one decision. The students simply wouldn't trust me." He nodded firmly. "My decision will stay. Class 605 is done with the newspaper."

He held up a copy of the laminated pledge. "And what is this?" he asked. "I found copies all over the school," he said. "It's so redundant!"

Nadia wanted to stay mad at Taylor, but she just couldn't, after all he'd been through.

Vikram—and all the other students—of course didn't know any of the background.

"It's just so unfair," he said. "Now we're right back where we were at the start of the semester, with that pathetic petunia."

"What are you going to do about it, Nadia?" asked Jason.

"Huh?" said Nadia. *Haven't I done enough?* "I wasn't planning on doing anything," she told her friends.

"Really?" said Chloe. "That doesn't sound like you, Nadia. You always speak up when something's not right."

Yeah, Nadia thought. *And look where that got us.*

But by dinner that night, Nadia's stomach was in knots.

"What's wrong, habibti?" asked her mother. "I thought you loved my meatloaf."

"I do," said Nadia. "I'm just not that hungry."

"Something's bothering you," said Baba. "Get it off your vest."

Nadia gave a wan smile. The newspaper and mascot stuff seemed so silly, so middle school drama-y, especially after saving Titi's life. Her parents would probably think she was being melodramatic. She should just get over it and move on. So why couldn't she?

"Nadia," Mama said. "I know sometimes it feels like your father and I are old and out of it, but we were kids once, too, you know. You can talk to us."

Nadia flinched. Khefren-slash-Taylor had said the same thing. She reached for the amulet out of habit, but her hands grasped on nothing—she and Titi had agreed to keep it locked in his desk for now. And with Khefren inside, Nadia hadn't wanted to wear it anyway.

All of a sudden, everything that happened the last four weeks—or almost everything—came spilling out.

"And now Principal Taylor canceled the mascot contest and the paper," she finished. "I don't know what to do."

Baba took a deep breath before answering.

"Oh, habibti," he said. "You've been through a lot. But I can see where your principal's coming from—"

Nadia gave Baba a look. Was he siding with Taylor?

"—but the truth is," Baba continued, "a good leader isn't afraid to change their mind when they learn new things or gain new perspective."

Mama nodded. "That's the only way the world moves forward. And how else are leaders going to learn new things or gain new perspective unless people speak up? When you see injustice, no matter what kind, you need to speak up and use your voice."

Nadia frowned. "But that's the thing. Every time I use my voice, it seems to backfire. The boring article, the whole mascot thing which turned into such a mess. And that horrible fake news article . . ."

"So the consequences of speaking up weren't exactly what you were expecting," offered Baba. "That doesn't mean you give up. You roll with the punches. You learn something new. And then you speak up again."

"Words are power, and in this country, everyone has the power to speak their mind," added Mama. "So if the newspaper and the mascot mean that much to you, find a way to say that so Principal Taylor will listen."

Words are power.

Nadia straightened up in her seat, an idea forming in her head.

As soon as they finished eating and she had loaded the dishwasher, she started a text to the Nerd Patrol and a handful of other people from the Sphinx Squad.

She was about to press send, but couldn't bring herself to do it.

She put her phone down and climbed into bed.

Nadia was still in a funk the next day. She didn't even react when Titi rolled into class driving a motorized Roman chariot.

Titi asked her to stay after the bell rang.

"Suffering scarabs, Nadia," he said. "Enough with the pouting. What's bothering you?"

Nadia took in Titi's face, so caring, so concerned. She suddenly felt terrible for ever doubting him, if only for a minute.

She confessed her moment of confusion, when she

thought Titi had set her up with that fake news article. "And Khefren didn't even use magic to make me mad at you. He just made me trust him, then used my doubts to try to turn me against you."

"Manipulation casts its own kind of spell, doesn't it?" Titi said, smiling gently at Nadia. "It's good you recognize that. Here's what I've learned over the millennia: Most people are good. But there are those like Khefren who take advantage of people and situations for their own gain. That's why you have to be savvy. Check your sources. Trust your gut."

Nadia's gut was telling her that she needed to do something to stand up to Taylor. To demand that they continue the mascot contest and the newspaper.

But she was tired. And every time she tried to send the text to her friends, she pictured Taylor. He'd been through so much. It didn't seem fair to put him through more. She told Titi all this.

"Oh, Nadia," Titi said. "Your empathy is one of the things I appreciate most about you. Taylor was an innocent victim in Khefren's scheme, but this is bigger than him, just like me going back to the palace after all those years away was about more than Khefren. And I wish I had done it sooner. Maybe Khefren wouldn't have risen to power the way he did. Maybe I wouldn't have been trapped in that amulet." He paused. "Of course, then I never would have met you. So never mind—I take it all back."

Nadia smiled.

"My point is," Titi continued, "you have an opportunity here. And unlike old Titi, if you speak up now, you'll show Taylor—and everyone—what's right, before things get too wrong."

Nadia took a deep breath. "Thanks, Titi, I don't know what I'd do without you." She gave him a hug. "Gotta run!" she said. It was time to text her friends.

Meet me at Ice Scream tomorrow at 2PM? I need to talk to you about something important.

Chapter Nineteen

Monday morning, Nadia and the rest of the crew from Ice Scream each showed up at school with a stack of home-printed newspapers.

Everyone had pitched in. Nadia, Sarah, and Adam each wrote an article. Vikram laid everything out. Mateo designed the name of their paper in fancy letters across the top: The Real Scoop. And Jason printed it up.

They handed the papers out in the hallways and passed them around at the beginning of each class. They even put some in the teachers' mailboxes. Nadia gave one to Mike in homeroom, then read her column one more time.

As a Matter of Fact

by Nadia Youssef

I'll put it to you straight—I published fake news. I did not mean to do it. I was under deadline, I was upset about the mascot contest, and I took the easy way out.

Of course, the "easy way out" often ends up making things harder. I wanted to forget the whole thing ever happened, and thought about not writing this piece because of that.

But I didn't hurt just myself. My newspaper classmates suffered because I made a bad decision. The Hawkeyes were hurt, too, and there was no reason for that. No reason for me to tear them down just so I could come out on top.

I started the mascot contest to bring our school together to fight for change against an outdated tradition. But when things got tough, I chose to go low instead of high. That was a mistake.

Most of us—probably all of us—make mistakes. Mistakes are good; they are how we learn. But we have to acknowledge them first. Only then can we move on.

But not everyone owns up to their mistakes. Sometimes, even the adults in our lives don't. Here's something I've learned this semester: *The people in charge are not always right.*

The mascot represents who we are. The newspaper is our voice. And while mistakes deserve consequences, taking away our ability to express who we are and what we believe should not be one of them.

Fellow students: It is our duty to speak up and demand what is right when our leaders lose their way. And if we change our thinking from "me against you" to "us against what's wrong," we will be unstoppable.

And *that* is a matter of fact.

Early Wednesday morning, the Bridget Mason Middle Schoolers certainly seemed unstoppable.

They gathered in front of the school and held signs that read SAVE OUR PAPER! NEW MASCOT NOW! And SPEAK UP AND SPEAK OUT!

And they chanted:

"What do we want? A new mascot!

When do we want it? Now!"

And . . .

"Two, four, six, eight, what do we appreciate?

Newsflash, Newsflash, *we want* Newsflash!

Why, why, why? Because it's really fly!

When, when, when? As soon as we can!"

Nadia stood on the steps and looked down at the students gathered below. Almost the whole school was there, protesting together. The jocks, the nerds, both types of goths, the rockers, and the artsy types, just to name a few.

Adam ran up to Nadia. "You're never gonna believe it. I was looking through my phone and I found a video from the food fight I never watched. One guess who threw that cheeseburger at you?"

"Well, first of all, it was coleslaw," Nadia said, a smile on her face. "And my guess is . . . Taylor-slash-Khefren?"

"You know it," Adam said.

Just then Nadia spotted Mr. Flores standing in the doorway. She and Adam walked over. "Hey, Mr. Flores!" she called.

"Hey, Nadia, Adam," he said, a bit shyly. His uniform glittered in the sunlight.

"Fancy," Nadia said, smiling.

Mr. Flores looked down, then scowled, brushing sparkles off his shirt. "Ferrari! He uses so much glitter. I'll never be free of it."

Nadia and Adam shared a look. So *that's* why Flores had a beef with Titi!

"I read the article you wrote, Nadia," said Mr. Flores, looking up. "It was good. Very honest."

"Thank you," said Nadia.

"I'm sorry that *Newsflash* got canceled. You know, I was a journalist back in Peru and I really loved seeing you young reporters at work."

Nadia grinned. "Really? That is super cool, Mr. Flores. I'd love to hear about your journalism experience. Hey, maybe you could ask Ms. Tovey if you could talk to our class sometime." She paused. "Even without the paper, we can keep learning about journalism."

Mr. Flores smiled back. "That would be an honor."

Adam spoke up. "I've been meaning to ask you something, Mr. Flores. You didn't have anything to do with that No-Littering Pledge, did you?"

Mr. Flores shook his head. "Nope. And it was Principal Taylor's idea to put it by the garbage cans, too." He shrugged. "I'm not sure I'll ever figure him out. He's an odd one."

"You don't know the half of it," Nadia said. "But I have

a good feeling that things will be calmer around here going forward."

"Sounds good to me," said Mr. Flores. He headed back into the school, and Nadia and Adam joined the crowd at the bottom of the steps.

"Hello, hello, can you hear me?" said a loud, familiar voice a moment later.

Adam pointed back up the steps. Principal Taylor was holding up a megaphone.

"Hello, students," he said. "You've given me a lot to think about this week. I've thought long and hard. And I've decided . . . *Newsflash* can continue."

Nadia practically jumped with joy. Principal Taylor was drowned out by the students' cheering and had to wait until it died down to continue.

"Hold on, hold on," Principal Taylor said. "I'm not done! I've decided it's time for a new mascot, too, if that's what you would like. I will always have a place in my heart for the petunia, but I realize that time passes and tastes change. This is not about me; this is about you, the student body, and you have a right to a mascot you believe in."

The cheering continued, Nadia's the loudest of all.

Taylor held up a white envelope. "So inside this envelope are the results of the mascot vote that would have been shared at the spirit rally last week, had things not gotten so . . . spirited." He ripped open the envelope with a flourish. "And the winner is . . ."

Nadia held her breath as Taylor pulled out the results.

"Huh?" His brow furrowed. "The blobfish?"

Nadia's jaw dropped as the students around her went wild. She turned around to congratulate Vikram. He was pumping his fist and jumping up and down.

"YES! YES! EMBRACE THE BLOB!" he shouted.

Vikram turned to Nadia, his eyes shining. "My Blobster stickers were apparently quite popular. I heard some kids made him a write-in candidate," he explained. "But I didn't know it was that many kids!"

Nadia chuckled. Only Vikram could get a whole school behind a mascot as strange as a blobfish. But it was certainly going to be entertaining. And who knew? Maybe inspiring.

"Bridget Mason Blobfish! Bridget Mason Blobfish!" the crowd chanted.

"We will debut the mascot at the big game against Westside Middle on Saturday!" Principal Taylor said.

"I volunteer to be the mascot! I volunteer! I've already started on the costume!" Vikram shouted.

Nadia left Vikram to his mascot aspirations and she, Titi, and Adam headed inside to Titi's classroom. There was still the unfinished business of what to do with the hippo amulet.

"I present to you," Titi said, "The Box." And there, on a pedestal next to his desk, sat a special container that he had built. It was made of thick, clear plexiglass so they'd still be able to see and admire the hippo. Nadia took a closer look. There were small pictures and hieroglyphs drawn around the edge—little bits of extra magic to keep the magician contained. There was also a huge lock so the amulet could never be removed. And there were holes built into the box so sound could pass through.

"Now Khefren can listen to me teach every single day for the next three thousand years," Titi said.

"Holy hippopatami!" cried Nadia, in a flawless impression of Titi. "It's perfect, but—" She paused for dramatic effect, trying to keep a straight face. "I have a confession to make. When I sent Khefren back to the amulet,

I added a little something to the spell. Something we hadn't talked about."

Titi's face went white. "What did you do, Nadia?!" There was panic in his voice.

"Don't worry," Nadia said. "Khefren is safe in the hippo. But *where* in the hippo? *Ye nih*—I mean, *you need* to figure it out."

Adam crinkled up his face for a moment, concentrating. Then his eyes lit up.

"You didn't!" he said to Nadia.

Nadia turned to Titi. "I snuck a 'ye nih' in when I sent Khefren back. 'Ye nih' backward is . . ."

Now it was Titi's turn to scrunch up his face.

"Heavens to Mentuhotep, Nadia! You sent Khefren to the hippo hiney? For me?"

"What are friends for?" asked Nadia. She smiled. "I guess your old friend got a *bum* rap!"

"He was left *behind*!" said Adam.

Titi sniffed and wiped an imaginary tear from his eye. "It's a *booty*-ful thing, what friends can accomplish when they work together, isn't it?"

The bell for the start of class rang.

"And now," Nadia said, "sadly, these jokes must come an end—a *rear end*!"

Epilogue

The magician banged his fist on the wall of the amulet. Curse that terrible teacher, the know-it-all girl (hello, most of her facts were no fun at all) and that strange backward-talking boy!

But they had to know that a magician as powerful as himself would not be kept in a hippopotamus's behind for long. His magic was stronger than ever. This was a temporary situation, he was sure of it. He just needed some time to think.

He stuck his fingers in his ears and hummed the jingle for Scarabs R Us to drown out the voices of his captors, but it was no use. Why, oh why, had he chosen to shape-shift into a crocodile?! That annoying nut obsession he had after turning into a squirrel should have taught him a lesson. But sadly, it had not.

He banged his fist on the wall again, wondering if the girl knew this "fun fact," which would mock him forever: Crocodiles have excellent hearing.

About the Authors

Photo by Andrew Frasz

Bassem Youssef, aka the Jon Stewart of the Arab World, was a heart surgeon in his home country of Egypt before becoming the host of *AlBernameg*, the first political satire show in the Middle East. He has appeared on *The Daily Show*, *The Late Show with Stephen Colbert*, and other late-night shows, and was also featured in TIME 100, *Time* magazine's list of the one hundred most influential people in the world. He lives in Los Angeles with his family.

Photo by Cindy Johnson Photography

Catherine R. Daly has written many books for young readers, including *What Was the Age of Exploration?*, the Petal Pushers middle-grade series, and the Disney Fairies chapter books *Prilla and the Butterfly Lie* and *Four Clues for Rani*. She lives in New York City with her family and their fiesty Boston terrier, Jack.

About the Artist

Photo courtesy of the artist

Douglas Holgate is the illustrator of the *New York Times* bestselling series The Last Kids on Earth by Max Brallier, as well as the Planet Tad series, the Cheesie Mack series, and many other books for young readers. He has illustrated countless comics, as well as the graphic novels *Wires and Nerve, Volume One* by Marissa Meyer and *Clem Hetherington and the Ironwood Race*, cocreated with writer Jen Breach. Douglas lives in Melbourne, Australia, with his family and a large dog who is possibly part polar bear.

31901068359282